DEKKER'S DEMONS

BLOOD RUN

CALIBER
B O O K S

Also from ALAN CAILLOU

CABOT CAIN Series
    Assault on Kolchak
    Assault on Loveless
    Assault on Ming
    Assault on Agathon
    Assault on Fellawi
    Assault on Aimata

TOBIN'S WAR Series
    Dead Sea Submarine
    Terror in Rio
    Congo War Cry
    Afghan Assault
    Swamp War
    Death Charge
    The Garonsky Missile

MIKE BENASQUE Series
    The Plotters
    Marseilles
    Who'll Buy My Evil
    Diamonds Wild

IAN QUAYLE Series
    A League of Hawks
    The Swords of God

DEKKER'S DEMONS Series
    Suicide Run
    Blood Run

The Charge of the Light Brigade
A Journey to Orassia

Rogue's Gambit
Cairo Cabal
Bichu the Jaguar
The Walls of Jolo
The Hot Sun of Africa
The Cheetahs
Joshua's People
Mindanao Pearl
Khartoum
South from Khartoum
Rampage
The World is 6 Feet Square
The Prophetess
House on Curzon Street

DEKKER'S DEMONS: BLOOD RUN
Book Two

Cover art by Maxim Apryatin

For further information visit the Caliber Comics website:
www.calibercomics.com

CHAPTER 1

It was to be a terrifying day for all of them.

It started off well enough; a fine Parisian morning in July of 1942, sun shining brightly as they drove through the beautiful forest of Fontainebleau, with its oaks and wild pine trees, spruce, chestnut, and birch towering everywhere. The chalk knolls of the forest, thickly covered with heather and gorse and ferns, were spectacular.

This was German-occupied France, and the famous forest, with its hidden airstrips and firing ranges, was infested with German troops. But Josh Dekker, American ex-Marine, ex-parachutist (the Hundred and First, the finest fighting outfit since the days of Julius Caesar), was in the uniform of a Gestapo corporal and driving a stolen German O.M truck. At the moment, he hadn't a care in the world.

Dekker's knowledge of German was almost nil, and his French was abominable, though it was improving fast. But the language problem was solved by Ira Watslaw, the Polish Jew who spoke not only impeccable German, but six or seven other languages as well. He was in the truck's cab with Josh, and he was dressed as a Gestapo colonel, a uniform not to be argued with.

(This was why Josh Dekker had chosen to masquerade as a corporal, even though he was the definitive head of this team of commando freebooters; in the presence of a colonel, a mere corporal would not be expected to dare open his lower-class mouth in the case of an emergency.)

"You do all the talking, as usual," he had said to Ira. "I'm just your driver."

5

Sandwiched between them was one of the most fascinating young women history had ever been privileged to see.

Her name was Jill Magran, and she was French-American, born in St. Lô, Normandy, and brought up since her childhood in the States. As a young girl, she was an athlete and a gymnast. As a young woman in her twenties, she had been an instructor in un-armed combat in Cairo, Egypt, to General Charles de Gaulle's Free French Forces. Under her guidance were young expatriate soldiers who wanted nothing more out of life than to get their hands on the German soldiers who had desecrated, with the most horrific rape and pillage, a country they all loved. Jill Magran taught these boys to cut off the Germans' balls before slicing their throats.

Now, she was one of Josh Dekker's team, and she liked to tell him as often as possible, "I'm the best fucking man you've got, you sonofabitch, and don't ever forget it."

They'd first met back home when Josh, at the age of eighteen, had seduced her in the back of his father's car. She'd been three years younger, and the pregnancy had shocked her, driving her to find out just how to get rid of it and then to abort herself with a wooden spoon. Then she left him forever. Forever, that is, until the unexpected meeting ten years later in Cairo while Josh Dekker, pulled out of the Hundred and First by one Wild Bill Donovan, who was head of the newly formed and still immature Office of Strategic Services.

Sometimes, Jill hated his guts. But more frequently, she longed for his strong arms crushing her naked body to his, to feel him driving into her furiously, both of them living only for the moment, knowing that the next few hours might bring certain agonizing death if they were ever captured; the Gestapo was not exactly famous for its tenderness to captured American commandos.

Sitting beside him now in the stolen truck, she was in her favorite cover, as a hooker picked up on rue Godot de Mauroy, where all the most expensive ladies hung out, a cover that had served her very well in the past. She wore a mauve cashmere sweater two sizes too small for her with nothing underneath it except herself, her nipples pointedly defined, an impossibly short-short skirt, and spike heels a mile high. Only once, through four roadblocks since they'd left the city itself, had her presence in the truck been questioned.

Mostly, the roadblocks had been manned by the lesser ranks, but at one of them there'd been a lieutenant, young and zealous. Standing smartly to attention in the presence of Ira Watslaw's Gestapo colonel, and trying to show off his devotion to the rules, he had barked: "With respect, Herr *Oberst*, does the woman have the necessary travel permit?"

Ira Watslaw roared: "None of your damn business, *Leutnant*! Now open that damned barrier or you'll be a corporal tomorrow!"

"*Jawohl*, Herr *Oberst*."

As the Lieutenant turned away, the Polish Jew went into one of his favorite acts: He said sternly: "Halt!"

The lieutenant stopped and turned back. "Sir?"

"When you address a senior officer of the Gestapo, scum, you are expected to give the requisite salute."

Hastily, the Lieutenant raised his right arm and shouted: "Heil Hitler!"

"Again."

There was the click of heels, the raised right arm.

"Heil Hitler! Heil Hitler!"

"Good," Ira Watslaw said calmly. "You may now raise the barrier with the same urgency. And if I remember to do so, I will commend you to your Commanding Officer."

In moments, they were on their way again, and Josh Dekker said patiently: "One of these days, you Polish prick, you're going to push your luck a little too far."

Ira laughed. "Don't count on it," he said. "The one thing the German army understands is the voice of authority. I just like to gratify my sense of the ridiculous once in a while. God knows there's little enough to laugh at in Europe these days."

Dekker and his group were on their way to check out a secondary safe-house in the forest which their friends in the French Resistance had discovered; there were never enough hiding places to scuttle away to when the going got rough. The safest of them all had been in Paris, but a drunken German officer had stumbled on it by accident, and though Josh Dekker had quickly, skillfully, and silently killed him, there was always the one chance in a hundred that he had not been along, so he had given the order, "Until we're sure, fellas, we evacuate, and at once."

They came to the intersection of the Circular Route, and Josh Dekker began to swing the wheel round to the right. Jill said urgently, "No, we go straight on here! We turn off onto Route fifty-eight at Fontainebleau itself...?"

"The Circular Route will take us where we're going," Josh said, "and it's much more scenic."

He looked at her. "Besides which, there's been a Mercedes on our tail for the last ten minutes, hadn't you noticed? I just want to make sure..."

Jill turned to stare into the rearview mirror. "Oh God...the black one?"

"The Gestapo always chooses black, it seems to suit them."

Ira Watslaw nodded. "Ever since we left Chailly-en-Bierre," he said calmly. "Five men on board, in civilian clothing. Sometimes only one or two car-lengths behind us, sometimes five or six. But always hanging onto our tail."

"Pass the word to the fellows in the back," Josh Dekker said tightly, and Jill Magran turned and slid back the window. "Hugh?"

Hugh Black was there at once, older than the others, a British ex-Major from Eighth Army Intelligence, cashiered for passing bad checks in Cairo's Birka, the brothel area. Black was a weapons expert and a thoroughly nice old man.

He said, not waiting for Jill to speak: "Yes, we know, we're being followed, a big black Mercedes. I can drop some *plastique* explosives in its path if it ever gets near enough, but it's staying a careful two or three car-lengths behind us. And I honestly don't want to blow up some innocent French family off on a picnic in the forest. I mean, it's hardly the gentlemanly thing to do, is it?"

"Del and Mike...?"

"Del is watching through the back canvas, and Mike is fast asleep. What else?"

Del Adam, a Shakespearean actor stranded in Cairo by the war, was a blade-man now. He'd forsaken his hash and oil-running operation from Lebanon through Palestine and into Egypt, to join up with Dekker's little commando. (He'd tried to enlist within twenty-four hours of America's entry into the conflict, but had been turned down because of his criminal background.) He was deadly with any one of the three knives he habitually concealed on his body, each one of them honed to a perfection of sharpness; his best could slice a falling hair in two.

Mike Homer was the young American pilot who had once, at the age of eighteen, flown his homemade aircraft clear across the Caribbean Sea to Venezuela, walking away from the crash landing. Anything mechanical, Mike Homer could fix, and put to good use.

"We just might be in trouble, Hugh," Josh Dekker said grimly. "If we are, then we use the silenced Anderson guns and our knives, no loud noises, now. This forest is filled with Germans, let's not invite them down on our heads, okay?"

"Whatever you say, Josh. And do I have to wake up poor Mike? He's sleeping like a child, it seems a shame to disturb his rest..."

Josh Dekker sighed, and turned back to his driving.

"It won't be just the five of them in that Mercedes," Jill Magran said. "They'll have backup, without a doubt."

He nodded. "I know it. Sooner or later, we're going to find a roadblock up ahead. Unless we look for the paths instead of the main roads. And that's what we're doing now."

He was right. But then Josh Dekker was almost never wrong.

It was only three hours before that General Hans von Finstadt had been awoken with most appalling news.

He was a tired old man in his early seventies, and he was head of the Gestapo in Paris. He was a man, surprisingly, of very gentle feelings, who nonetheless headed the most brutally repressive military organization Europe had ever known.

With a casual flourish of his pen, he could callously sign away the lives of a hundred French hostages. And yet, he was a sincere family man, deeply devoted to his children and his grandchildren (though not to his wife, whom he actively hated), and always watchful over their well-being.

And in bed with his mistress, he could be brought to tears very readily by the knowledge of his near impotence.

A lieutenant of the Gestapo came to him at his apartment in the

Georges Cinq Hotel, and he said furiously to the guard on the door, a very young sergeant; "I don't care if he's on top of his damned whore! Wake the General up, man, or by God, you'll be a private soldier tomorrow, and cleaning out latrines!"

The Sergeant was very unsure. He said, stammering, "With respect, Herr *Leutnant*, my orders are that the Herr General and his lady were not to be disturbed."

"God damn your eyes, man! Stand out of my way!"

He shoved the Sergeant aside and hammered on the door, and in a moment, the sleepy voice in there answered peevishly: "Yes? Who is it?"

The Lieutenant snapped automatically to attention, and he said, raising his voice: "*Leutnant* Mansfeld, Herr General! A matter of some importance!"

He was one of the General's aides, and he expected immediate attention, but it was a very long time before the bolts were thrown and the door was opened, to disclose the old General's skinny and anemic body, white as an aspirin and wrapped in a sheet that was hardly whiter.

He said, scratching at his belly, "I hope this truly is important, Mansfield."

"With respect, Sir, I felt that you would not wish to hear this from a stranger."

The General held open the door and stepped back. "Come in then, *Leutnant*. But keep your voice down, my lady is still asleep."

"Of course, Herr General."

Automatically, his eyes went to the huge four-poster bed.

Madame Yvonne Fremont was lying there, barely covered, her eyes closed. She was von Einstadt's longtime mistress whom he loved dearly, largely because she was a woman who, with her hands, and lips, and her thighs, could bring an astonishing frequency of orgasms from his frail white flesh. Many years ago, as a virile and handsome young Major, the General had been very much a ladies' man and he could never quite forgive a relentless God for taking that virility from him. But in Yvonne Fremont, he had found a woman who seemed able to recapture some of his lost youth for him, even though it usually took her a great deal of time and effort.

She was French, and proprietress of a fabulous restaurant called Le Cochon Qui Rit, the Laughing Pig. It was a place that in war-torn Paris still managed to serve excellent food from the black market, largely because it was where the senior ranks of the Gestapo liked to eat.

Yvonne Fremont was in her early forties, still firm breasted and very voluptuous; she was highly skilled in the arts of physical love. On the night of their first assignation, she had brought this seventy-year-old skeleton of a once-strong man, who had not enjoyed an orgasm in more than five years, to a peak of excitation and beyond. She managed to do this three times in a twelve-hour orgy of the most unusual forms of sexual activity. A relationship had been quickly cemented; Yvonne Fremont had become his twice-a-week mistress.

She was tall, slender, long legged, and slim hipped, with a high forehead over dark and probing eyes and finely carved features. She was a splendid woman to look at and to sleep with, a woman not only of marked sensuality but of high intelligence, too.

And she was also a senior officer in the French Resistance, a spy in the very heart of the German High Command; a woman to be reckoned with, indeed.

Now, the General said wearily, wrapping his sheet more tightly about him, "And what is it, *Leutnant*, that demands my attention at two in the morning? What is it I would not 'wish to hear from a stranger?' You speak in riddles, Mansfeld, and I am a plain, blunt man, as you must know. I am impatient of riddles."

The lieutenant said quietly: "Your grandson, Sir. Lieutenant Heinrich von Einstadt. He has been killed, Sir, murdered by a commando that raided our armory in Dempierre, where he was the Officer in Command. It pains me to be the bearer of bad news."

"Oh God..."

The General felt the blood draining from his face. Heinrich was the favorite of all his grandsons. Twenty-three years old, he was surely headed for promotion, not only because of his family, but also because he had proved himself to be singularly adept at inventing new forms of persuasion for the captured enemies of the Reich.

It was Heinrich who had dreamed up the idea of packing kerosene-soaked rags around the spread thighs of a Resistance prisoner, male or female, and then leaving a half-inch of burning candle balanced there to give them an hour or more of thought and anticipatory terror before the slow flames took over.

In spite of his age—perhaps because of it—the General was not a man who easily lost control of himself. He turned away to hide the shame of the tears in his eyes, and he said: "Did he at least die bravely, Mansfeld?"

"He did, Sir," the Lieutenant said promptly. "They threw a dozen hand grenades, of a type we have never seen before, into the guardroom, killing almost everyone there. Your grandson, Sir, survived the initial attack, though he was gravely wounded. Hurt as he was, he led a charge against the invaders..."

"Yes, yes, yes," the General said wearily. His voice was very tired; he knew that Heinrich was not exactly a hero. "I'm sure of it."

He took a long, deep breath. "And what do we know about the attacking commando? The Resistance, I assume?"

"No, Sir. It was an American commando unit, led by a man named Dekker. I think you may have heard of him."

"Josh Dekker," the General said tightly. "Yes, I've heard of him. The man's a maniac, a monster inviting slow death with every move he makes."

"It was he, Sir," Mansfeld said, "who fired the fatal shot, with a silenced pistol, to your grandson's forehead."

The pain was awful. The General had a daughter whom he had adored, Heinrich's mother. On her way to Lyons one recent day with her Gestapo-Major husband, their car had been machine-gunned by a group of the Resistance commanded by no less a personage than the legendary Jean Moulin himself, a patriot of the most fearsome potential, soon to become head of all the Resistance groups in occupied France. Heinrich, (the real target of the assault) was supposed to have been with them, but he'd simply forgotten the rendezvous, and they'd left without him.

There was a dazed and distant kind of look in the General's red-rimmed eyes, and he said, his voice filled with his anguish, "This man Dekker has been a thorn in our side for long enough, Mansfeld, and I want him *found*. I want him brought to me, still alive. Hurt, incapacitated, close to death—I don't care! Just as long as he's still breathing, still able to suffer what I'll do to him. You understand what I'm saying, *Leutnant?*"

"I understand, Sir. And I'm happy to tell you that we are closing in on him now."

"You are?"

"Yes, Sir. When the raid was over and they had collected all the ammunition they came for, one of our men was lying in a culvert, more dead than alive. Just a sergeant, but he has, it seems, a certain working knowledge of English. And he heard one of them say: 'We'll need a German truck to take us to the forest.' Moments later, they had stolen one of our vehicles, and were heading south. *South?* And to *a forest?* It can only mean Fontainebleau, Herr General."

The General nodded. "Agreed. And what steps have you taken?"

Mansfeld smiled thinly. "Five of my men are following them at this moment, Herr General. Behind the Mercedes, there is a school bus containing twenty-seven of our paratroopers. And behind that, there are three heavily armed personnel carriers, keeping their distance but still in radio contact with the Mercedes."

"And how many are there in this commando?"

"There seem to be only six, Herr General. One of them is a woman, and our information seems to indicate that she is French-American, by name Jill Magran, born in a place called Périers, near St. Lô."

The General said harshly, "Her parents? Her family?"

"We are looking for them now, Sir," Lieutenant Mansfeld said. "When we find them, they will, of course, be taken care of."

"And this Jill Magran herself?"

"Young, it seems," the Lieutenant said, "and she is constantly described as very beautiful. And moreover, quite efficient at what she does."

"Beautiful..." the General echoed. "When I have finished with her, her beauty will be a thing of the past."

He went to the dresser where the bottles and the glasses were set out, and poured himself half a tumbler of Johnny Walker, and as he drank, he said viciously: "A lesson in feminine psychology for you, Mansfeld. For a beautiful woman, a dagger thrust into her vagina is of far less consequence than the removal of her nose with a sharp razor, did you know that? They *guard* their good looks, the most important, in their minds, of all their attributes. And what is important for them, is important for us. We must always know their weakness, and profit by our knowledge."

"Yes, Sir, I'm aware of it."

"It's part of what made the Gestapo strong, Mansfeld! Any idiot can tear off their fingernails, but it's not enough! We have a duty to take that feminine psychology into account too."

"Yes, Sir. You are right, of course, as always. And you have my promise. Sooner or later, I will bring this woman to you."

"And Dekker too."

"And Dekker too, very soon now. Their capture is assured."

The General, in a moment of weakness, poured another Johnny Walker and handed the glass to the Lieutenant.

He said sternly, "We will drink together, Mansfeld, like the good friends we are, to the memory of my beloved grandson Heinrich. And you will see to it that he is buried with full military honors, as befitting a hero of the Third Reich."

"I have already made the arrangements, Sir," Lieutenant Mansfeld said.

He raised his glass. "To the honored memory of *Leutnant* Heinrich von Einstadt, scion of an ancient and honorable German family, who died most bravely in the course of his honorable duty, a soldier to the last..."

"To Heinrich..."

The General tossed back his drink and hurled His glass into the corner, where it shattered against the wall. And he said coldly, "Now bring me Dekker. I want his still-living head on a silver platter, and the woman's too. Both of them still alive and capable of learning the extent of my fury, you understand me?"

"I understand you perfectly, Sir," Mansfeld said, "and I assure you—we can take them now whenever we wish. We are holding off for only one reason."

"Which is?"

"The expectation, Herr General, that they will be heading for their safe-house, which I would dearly like to find. And in the hope,

14

moreover, that they will lead us to the man known as Lievre."

"Ah. You're a good man, *Leutnant*, and the badges of rank of a Captain might be within your grasp now. Dekker and his damned crew. And Lievre too? That's a very considerable prize."

Le Lievre, the Hare.

He was commander of Group 47 of the French Resistance, with Paris and its immediate surroundings as his exclusive mandate; a wily, devious, and suspicious sort of man, tough as a hunk of shrapnel; he had been fighting the hated Germans for two years now, ever since the surrender of the French forces. He was second in importance, perhaps, only to the legendary Jean Moulin himself, and like that charismatic bureaucrat-turned-soldier he was deeply concerned with bringing together under one command the various—and often mutually hostile—factions of what was loosely known as the Resistance.

He was also a man upon whom Josh Dekker had to depend quite heavily from time to time. But Josh Dekker knew that no man could be trusted forever.

The Germans had already learned that Frenchmen could be found, and recruited to Nazi service, who felt very strongly that what their beloved country needed more than anything else, was the Germanic concept of law and order.

The dreaded *Milice*—a body of French fascists put together by the occupying German Army to root out the underground and destroy it—was still in its formative stages.

But a handful of these turncoats had already succeeded in infiltrating *la Résistance*, sometimes at its highest levels.

The following morning, in accordance with the orders of General Hans von Einstadt, one hundred and fifty French hostages were executed.

CHAPTER 2

Josh Dekker swung his heavy truck onto a narrow footpath through the dense shrubbery, the detailed map he had studied so carefully deeply etched into his mind. The heavy vehicle was crashing its own way through, bending saplings over, breaking off the branches that were closing in around them as they penetrated deeper and deeper. But five hundred yards or so farther on, he knew, there was a much better track that led to one of the secondary roads.

Jill Magran said sarcastically, "You do realize that if we run into trouble here, there's no way you can make a U-turn on this track? Did that occur to you?"

Josh felt his temper rising. He said testily: "It did. And did it *occur* to you that they've got us hemmed in here?"

"You can't be sure of that..."

"Oh yes I can! There's not only the Mercedes. Back on the road, there was a school bus—a school bus! Only, I got a brief glimpse of it, and it's filled with German troops."

"Oh, God..."

"Oh, God is right. They can take us any time they want, so why haven't they done just that?"

Not waiting for her reply, even if she had one, he said, "It means they're hoping we'll lead them to the safe-house. They've been keeping their distance, so that we won't catch on we're being followed. But now that we've turned off into...into this deathtrap, they'll realize they've been spotted. So they'll be closing all the exits now."

He turned his head and shouted: "Hugh!"

Hugh Black was there at once, sticking his terribly British head

16

through the dividing window, and Josh Dekker: said, "I can't see a goddamn thing in the rearview mirrors now. What happened to the Mercedes?"

"Well," the British ex-Major said, "you can't really expect a car like that to follow us here, it's not exactly an off-road vehicle, is it? But at the speed you're doing now; they're probably following us on foot, panting. In any case, dear boy, if you take my advice you'll dump this bloody truck at the first opportunity, so that we can all proceed on foot too. We'll make smaller targets, don't you know?"

It was a course that was slowly being forced on them, like it or not, and Josh said grimly, "We're about four miles from the safe-house, and I don't want to get any closer. If we have to leave the truck and run, we're bound to get separated, so that's where we meet."

"'If.'" Hugh Black echoed, "'If' my arse. I give us about ten more minutes before we have to go just that."

"And no one goes near the house till after dark. Too many binoculars in the Gestapo tool kit, just...watching. And do me a favor, Hugh. We went to a great deal of trouble to pick up one hell of a lot of ammunition. I don't want to hand it back to them."

"You got it."

"And whatever has to be left behind, Hugh, we need your pouch."

"I don't even go to bed without it."

Hugh's ten minutes was far too optimistic, and before they had gone half a mile there was a barrier of rocks and branches thrown across the narrow path, manned by twenty or thirty German troops, four heavy machine guns aimed in their direction.

And Josh Dekker slid to a halt and shouted, "Out! Everybody out!"

The bullets tore into the truck, but they were aimed low. *I want them alive*, the General had said.

The truck had bulldozed its way through the heavy bushes, the saplings, the closely packed trees, and had finally come to an up-ended stop in a deep ditch.

And the ditch was to be their salvation.

All six of them leaped down, and they ran for their lives.

And ninety seconds later, the truck blew up behind them, all its heavy load of looted ammunition exploding from a couple of Hugh Black's sophisticated *plastiques*.

Josh Dekker was a natural born commander of men—and women—who were as reckless as he was.

And as a good commander, it was part of his philosophy that he would not waste lives through unnecessary heroics. On his frequent lectures to his group, he would say sourly, "A dead fucking hero isn't that much use to the war effort, so don't anyone feel bad about it if we have to run, once in a while. When the odds get to be ridiculous, that's what we do—we *run*. And we'll all still be alive to hit back, hard, when the odds are more in our favor."

They ran for their lives, among the shadows of the forest, searching out the gullies which might give them shelter from the bullets of more than thirty machine pistols that were spraying the foliage like water out of a hose, very many more of them moving up now.

The Germans also had the new infantry 120mm mortar which had just recently replaced the less efficient *Granarwerfer Kurz*, and was infinitely more deadly; the bushes were erupting with iron fragments that clipped their way through the trees with a vicious, incisive sound that was the threat of instant mutilation or death.

Hugh Black found himself lying close by Dekker, and he said mildly, "Bit of a sticky wicket, isn't it?"

"Not a nice situation to be in," Dekker said, "if that's what you mean."

"And the wind's behind us, had you noticed?"

"No, I hadn't."

"Slight, but enough for what I have in mind."

"If you have some crazy idea for getting us out of this, Hugh..."

"It so happens that I have twenty-two miniature magnesium bombs in my backpack," said Hugh Black, a man who knew more about recondite weaponry than any ten men in the whole of war-torn Europe. "Do you think the French would mind if I were to set their beautiful Fontainebleau forest on fire? I worry about that."

18

"Then *stop* worrying, you goddam limey. And yes, the wind's behind us. Where's Jill, for Christ's sake?"

The bullets and the mortar fragments were stinging around them, heavier now.

"She was right beside me only moments ago. God knows where she is now."

"Del! Ira? Mike...?"

"Del's gone into their lines with a knife in each hand, and Ira's right beside him with his Anderson gun. Mike? Mike must find all this terribly boring; he's probably asleep under a bush somewhere, waiting for all the excitement to die down."

He was delving into his pack and coming up with the little magnesium bombs, laying them out in meticulous precision on the earth in front of him.

This was July of a very hot summer, and the brush around them was dry as straw. Hugh scratched the firing surfaces of the bombs one by one, and hurled them out into the woods. And in moments, the forest was in flares.

"The wind can change, Josh," Hugh Black said. "It's to our advantage to get the hell out of here as best we can..."

"Not until I make sure Jill's okay. Where was she when you last saw her?"

Hugh pointed. "A hundred yards back there."

The firing had almost stopped now. It was as though the Germans had suddenly remembered their obligation to take the prisoners alive. Hugh and Josh scrambled on all fours along the gully in the eerie silence, and pulled up short.

There was the sound of coarse laughter only twenty or thirty yards to one side of them. Dekker signaled, and flat on their bellies, their silent guns ready, they snaked their way up the bank toward the sound, dragging their way cautiously under the foliage.

And then, peering through the bushes, they saw them.

Jill was there, lying still and silent on the ground. Her sweater, heavily soaked in blood, had been ripped wide open, and one breast was covered in blood too, the other delicately white and pristine.

Her skirt had been pulled up to her waist, and Josh saw her black silk panties lying on the grass there, carelessly tossed aside.

With her, there were three German soldiers, a Sergeant and two troopers; the Sergeant had handed his Schmeisser to one of his men. He was kneeling between her spread thighs, his trousers undone and pushed down to his knees. The two men were giggling like foolish children, and the Sergeant said, like a very knowing man, "It's just as good when they're unconscious, even better, they don't try and scratch your eyes out."

He had pulled down his underpants, and his bare behind was white and pimply as he stretched himself carefully out on top of her, groping with his hands.

Controlling himself with an effort, Josh Dekker signaled quickly to Hugh, *You rake the one on the right.*

Aiming instinctively, he fired his Anderson at the soldier on the left, and saw him drop with a small red hole dead center in his forehead. He heard the soft *plop* of Hugh's gun beside him as the second man fell, and readied himself for the third.

The Sergeant was swinging around in shock, struggling to his feet, obscenely exposed as he groped desperately for one of the fallen guns.

Dekker shot him in the groin, two quick shots followed by one to the throat to silence the beginning scream of pain, and a final round to the head.

They ran to Jill, and at first sight it seemed that she was dead; could there be so much blood and still be life? Moaning, Josh dropped to his knees beside her and took her in his arms, clutching at her. He whispered: "My darling, my darling."

But Hugh Black, older by far and wiser, pushed him brusquely aside and said urgently, "Let me look, I'm better at these things than you are."

His mind dulled, Josh gave way to him, and Hugh said, his fingers probing, "A mortar fragment, I think, I can't be sure."

"She's dead, isn't she?"

"No, she's not. The bloods still pumping, and we've got to stop it. My pouch..."

As Josh found the first-aid kit, Hugh tore open the bloodied sweater, lifted the tight skirt up to her waist, delicately fingered her body, and said at last, "Yes, a mortar fragment. It caught her in the thigh, twisted on a bone, and came out again. It creased her breast, that's where most of the blood is coming from, and then nicked her shoulder as well."

Josh began the urgent bandaging, and Hugh found one of his little vials with their built-in needles.

"Procaine Hydrochloride," he said, "and I'm giving her a very heavy dose. It's not what she really needs, but it will keep her unconscious for several hours. Because, believe me, when she comes round that's going to *hurt*."

"Round up the boys," Josh said, and knew at once that it was a very foolish comment, knew that he wasn't thinking straight now.

Hugh took him up on it at once. "And you're going to carry her all the way to the safe-house? Through a forest that has a German machine gun under every bush? They won't all be on the other side of the fire, you know. So how are you going to defend yourself when you have to, with Jill in your arms? No. I'll be beside you, running interference, the boys can take care of themselves well enough. We move as close to east as we can now, we stick to one gully after another, we crawl and drag her when we have to, and you worry only about getting her to the safe-house. I'll worry about anyone who tries to stop us."

The forest was alive not only with the crackling of the flames but with the deadly sound of machine-gun bullets and mortars all around them. Just as Hugh had suggested, the enemy wasn't only on the other side of the fires, taking stronger hold now, but behind them as well, a maelstrom of viciously flying lead and iron.

There was a strange look in Josh Dekker's eyes, eyes that were moist as he picked Jill up into his arms and held her tightly. The British ex-Major, understanding that his friend and leader was in no state now to make decisions that would affect them all, said quietly, "You'll agree with me, Josh, I'm sure. I'll take over command now. All you have to concentrate on is Jill. Just leave the rest to me."

Dekker nodded blankly. "Sure. And I thank you, Hugh."

"So let's get going. Just remember that we won't be safe till it's dark, not even then."

* * *

21

There was a drill for circumstances like these, that Josh Dekker himself had set down when they had first parachuted into France; they adhered to it very closely now.

Hugh Black went ahead down the deep gully for five hundred yards to scout, while Josh lay under deep cover with the unconscious Jill still beside him. Then Hugh ran quickly back to give the all-clear signal that would signify a move forward till the next reconnaissance. And so it would go on, time after weary time.

Once, they were discovered by a patrol of three German paratroopers, their Schmeisser machine pistols at the ready, but not ready enough; three rapid shots from Hugh's almost deathly silent Anderson gun to three Nazi foreheads killed them all before they could loose off a single round and localize the search.

Once, they lay together in uncanny silence under the cover of tightly packed shrubbery while a passing patrol of a dozen men decided to take a break for sandwiches, wine from their water bottles, and cigarettes. Less than twenty feet away, Josh and Hugh lay still, scarcely daring to breathe. Josh's hand was at Jill's face, dreading the possibility of her sudden recovery and a consequent moan that would have betrayed them all. Even Hugh was worried, they were far too close to use the deadly grenades he carried, grenades of his own invention and manufacture.

They were the size and shape of figs, made of high explosive embedded with tiny steel three-pointed spikes, sharp as needles and no more than an eighth of an inch long; they had been tipped with Brazilian curare, and a scratch was enough, they were mortal within a range of fifty feet.

For nearly an hour they lay there in the most acute silence, listening for snatches of conversation.

Neither of them knew a great deal of German, and where was Ira Watslaw, the linguist, now that they needed him? But they could make out the intent of the words, even without an exact translation.

"We better find those American bastards, you know that? If not, we can forget about leave, we won't get a day off for the next twenty years... And how in hell are we supposed to take them alive?"

"Did you hear what the old man's going to do to the woman?"

"No." A coarse laugh then. "But I can guess."

"You crazy? The Herr General, whom God preserve, of course, is too old to interest himself in what she's got between her legs. No, I have it on the best authority, he's going for her face with a razor."

"And I wouldn't like to be in their leader's shoes. What's his name? Drekker?"

"No, Dekker."

But they were laughing at a not subtle joke; *dreck*, in German, meant shit.

"Herr Shitmaster," the same voice went on. "He was the guy who shot the Lieutenant. *Gott in Himmel*, he was the Herr General's own grandson! Half the Gestapo will be dreaming up stuff for *him* right now, all of them looking for promotion. Jesus Christ! The poor bastard..."

There was only the sound of eating and drinking for a few moments, and then someone said, "Like that guy the dogs got the other day?"

"Who was that?"

"The spy they picked up a week or so ago, he dropped right into the arms of one of our patrols, just outside Marlotte. Bastard killed five of them and got away, but once they got the Dobermans out...that was the end of it. He'd been wounded, so there was blood, what more can the dogs want? They found him the next night, hiding out in a cave."

Someone said, grumbling, "What's that got to do with Herr Shitmaster?" The answer came back at once.

"They gave me forty-eight hours of duty in Marlotte jail, and I saw this guy. Christ, they had him trussed up like a turkey, stark naked and hanging from the rafters by a rope around his ankles, down in the cellar. His mouth was taped shut, and there was a wire coming out of it."

The group humorist said, "Positive, or negative?" and they roared with laughter. "Positive!" the speaker said. "The negative wire was wrapped around his cock! And every once in a while, the Sergeant would throw the switch, off again, on again."

There was an audible shudder, "Christ, I can still hear him screaming. And I tell you...they'll have a lot worse than that for

Dekker. I wouldn't like the Gestapo to write me down as an enemy, thank God we're all on the right side."

"*Macht ist Recht,*" one of the others murmured. "Might is right. Yes, it's true, and let's be grateful for it."

An officer happened on them and berated them for wasting valuable minutes; in no time at all, the immediate and deadly danger of the patrol was gone.

And once, a solitary *Leutnant,* looking for his patrol, his blond hair singed by the forest fire, stumbled on them.

Hugh Black had a twinge of conscience here as he shot him between the eyes, because the young Lieutenant was drunk as a coot, and it didn't seem fair to take advantage of his condition.

But Jill was beginning, quite alarmingly, to recover, and was moaning quietly, a situation which meant trouble for all of them.

With the dead officer lying close by, Hugh said, startled, "Your Jill has more *resistance* than any ten women I know! The dose I gave her..."

He had one of his little vials there again, its needle deeply embedded in her behind. "There," he said. "if that doesn't hold her, I give up."

Her moaning stopped, and as he gathered her up again, that tough soldier Josh Dekker was openly crying; Major Hugh Black said patiently, "How many times do I have to tell you, Josh? She's going to recover, very soon now."

The comforting words meant nothing to Josh.

The darkness came, and they were well out of the area of immediate danger. Or so they hoped.

They finally reached a clearing in the forest, and there was a woodcutter's hut there, just one room, built of logs and offering no sign of life at all.

Hugh Black said quietly, "Stay here, in silence. They do say that time spent on reconnaissance is seldom wasted."

He crept forward on his belly toward the hut, leaving the safe cover of trees; before he had gone a hundred yards, a huge gross body dropped on him from an overhanging branch. There was a strong forearm across his throat, half strangling him; worse, there was a knife, glinting in the moonlight, poised above his face for the killing slash at his windpipe.

Hugh Black was in his early sixties, and this was apparently a young and powerful man. He twisted himself out from under and tried to bring his gun hand up. But there was a knee on his wrist, a foot in his groin, and he was powerless.

And then, the brutish face above him was suddenly wreathed in the world's widest grin, and a voice said in welcoming French: "Major Black? I am Roland, M'sieur Commandant, you know me, I think. I am with Lievre. Forgive me, I did not recognize you."

The pressures were suddenly released, and Hugh said wryly: "Roland. Yes, of course, I remember you well, I have Josh Dekker with me, and Jill Magran. She's been badly hurt. Do we have a doctor here?"

"We will find one."

"The others? Has anyone reported in?"

"They're all here, Del Adam, Mike Homer, and that Polish maniac Ira Watslaw. They're all waiting for you, worried about you."

"And Lievre?"

Roland grinned broadly. "Lievre is here too, where else would he be at a time like this? You've brought the whole German Army into the forest, my friend. And Lievre is a very angry man."

He slapped the ex-Major on the back. "Come, I'll help you with Jill."

And five minutes later, Josh Dekker was confronting the famous head of Group 47 of the Resistance; as Roland had suggested, Lievre was a very angry man indeed.

CHAPTER 3

Lievre was a most extraordinary man. In his early thirties, he had risen very rapidly in the ranks of the Resistance, after an extraordinary incident that had taken place within two or three weeks of the German occupation of Paris in June; 1940.

A very young man, blindfolded but still shouting imprecations at his tormenters, was tied to a street lamppost, and in full view of the passersby (part of the German philosophy of applied terror) was shot to death by a firing squad of three soldiers armed with Schmeisser machine pistols. This in itself was bad enough, and the victims last shout, *"Vive la France!"* was still ringing in Lievre's ears. What followed was even uglier. Four innocent civilians on the street had been hit by the casual bullets, and one of them was a young girl from his own neighborhood. She died of her wounds in Lievre's frantic arms.

Screaming out his fury, he had taken the pistol he kept in his belt (very many Frenchmen had armed themselves in those early days, not yet fully appreciating the great danger), and had killed the Sergeant in charge of the firing squad and two of its members before Lievre had fallen, himself grievously wounded. The blackness had come over him, and he'd been only half conscious of being dragged away by a very old man, old enough to be his grandfather. And then, in a darkened corridor, he heard a sad, dispirited voice coming to him out of the void. "You did well, boy. France, poor France, is crying out for men like you, men of conscience. But I must leave you now. I have no wish to be caught harboring a *résistant*."

It was part of the birth of the Resistance.

But for Alphonse Brousse de Grevy, who gave himself the code name le Lievre, the Hare, it was the beginning of a new career, with the solitary aim of killing Germans.

There was already Henri Frenay's *Libération Nationale*, and the Christian Democratic *Liberté*, and the left wing *Libération*, headed by an obstreperous journalist named Emmanuel d'Astier de la Vigerie, as well as a number of other budding resistance movements.

But le Lievre would have no part of them, he wanted to be his own boss. And so, he formed his own body of fighting men, which he called Group 47 after the first forty-seven patriots who joined him.

Now, his command had swollen to nearly two thousand men, widely scattered over Paris and its suburbs, held together by the tightest possible discipline.

And le Lievre was not a man to fool around with.

He said now, harshly, "So. It was a failed operation, again."

"I don't think I like that 'again' too much," Josh said, "It was a *partly* failed operation. We picked up Christ knows how much ammunition, mostly nine millimeter, which is what we need. But at least they didn't recover it."

"A very *small* victory," Lievre said:

"Yes. Now where the hell is that fucking doctor of yours?"

"He'll be here any minute now."

"I hope to God you're right, Lievre."

The woodcutter's hut that was ostensibly the safe-house had been turned down by Lievre. Instead, he had chosen a cave within sight of it, leaving the hut as a marker.

It was a cave within a cave, and for three nights, nearly a hundred men of his group had toiled at carving out a tunnel in its limestone walls to make a back door, an escape route that led to a deep fissure in the rocks some three hundred yards away; Lievre was not the kind of man to allow himself to be trapped in a hideout with no way out.

"Jill," Josh Dekker said. "Jill is all that matters now."

"Yes, I'll agree with you there."

She was lying on a palliasse on the floor of the candlelit cave, and Hugh Black, the next best thing to a medic, was crouched beside her, his hand at her breast and feeling for the heartbeat.

"I don't believe it," he said. "I'll suggest now that a wound like this would have killed an ordinary woman. But Jill's not *ordinary*, is she?"

The doctor arrived at last, a wise old man on his last legs who just didn't care anymore if the Gestapo might discover him treating their mortal enemies.

He produced his rusty needle and stitched up Jill's dreadful wounds. She recovered her consciousness in the middle of his ministrations, and bit her lip nearly through to drive away the awful pain.

She reached up and touched Josh on the cheek, and she whispered, "I never ever thought I'd be such a pain in the ass for you."

"Sshh. Don't talk now, just rest. Soon, you'll be right as rain. And there's only one more thing to be said."

"Which is?"

He leaned down and kissed her on the lips. "That I love you so very much, my darling."

Her voice was a whisper. "And I, you..."

"If anything ever happened to you..."

"I know. It's my constant fear for you too..."

"My sweetheart..."

"My love..."

Lievre said sourly, "If I may interrupt this great love affair for just a moment. There's a message for you, Josh. From Donovan."

Josh Dekker could only stare. "From Wild Bill?"

"From Colonel Donovan in Cairo. It's in your private code, I found I couldn't break it."

"L.M.T. Code," Dekker said, "the easiest code in the world to break. It just takes like six months for a simple message..."

He took the slip of squared paper that Lievre handed him, and stared at the first few groups of letters.23

0009 ITSBE NROPI KIOOL HUIES GRIPLX PRQAES...

"Christ," he said, "I've forgotten the key."

Jill looked up at Lievre, sure that she could not trust him with such vital information, and she whispered, "The ship was sinking..."

"Ah yes..."

He wrote down, "I have not yet begun to fight," the key to his private code.

The first symbol, 0009, meant that he had to begin with the ninth letter—the *Y* of the word *Yet*.

As he laid out the key, *Y.E.T.B.E.G.U.N.T.O.F.I.* and began filling in the squares, he muttered, "Goddamn Donovan must really need us now. And all I can say is—if he wants us to go to work for him again, he'd better get down on his fucking knees and *beg*. And I'll still say no."

It took him nearly fifteen minutes to decipher the message, and he studied it for a moment before he decided that there was nothing there at all that Lievre could not hear.

He looked down at Jill on the palliasse, and reaching out to touch her arm, he whispered: "This affects you too, my darling. It affects all of us."

Hugh Black was waiting; Del Adam, a little apart from them, was silently honing his favorite knife on the Arkansas stone he always carried. Ira Watslaw was watching and waiting; Mike Homer was fast asleep in a chosen corner. Josh Dekker read slowly:

DONOVAN TO DEKKER PERSONAL STOP OKAY YOU SONOFABITCH I NEED YOU NOW STOP MY AGENT FERRET WENT OFF THE AIR IMMEDIATELY ON DROP IT MEANS HE IS EITHER PRISONER OR DEAD STOP IF FORMER ESSENTIAL REPEAT ESSENTIAL HE BE RESCUED AT ONCE STOP OUR FRIENDS REFUSE TO HELP STOP DO THIS FOR ME AND ALL WILL BE FORGIVEN MESSAGE ENDS.

He paced up and down for a moment, thinking deeply, and Lievre said at last, a little dryly, "I don't suppose you'd care to share that message with me?"

Dekker shrugged. "No reason why my friends shouldn't see it. Provided you tell me why it is you don't want to help out."

He handed the slip of paper over and waited. Lievre said at last, scowling, "I did *not* refuse to help."

He sighed. "Eight nights ago, this man Ferret was supposed to drop to us, fifteen miles south of here. It was a hell of a night, no moon, and pissing down with rain. We had trouble, a lot of trouble, with the fires for the letter of the day—"

"You mean you never heard of magnesium flares?"

"We don't normally carry them," Lievre said angrily. "The storm took us by surprise. We heard what I'm sure was his plane, but never saw it, it seemed to be off course quite a bit, and the *Bosches* were firing at it with everything they've got. And it just...disappeared."

"Crashed?"

"I don't think so. Even if we didn't hear it, we'd have found out the next day for sure. We assumed be couldn't find the dropping-ground and turned back, but then..."

He watched the doctor at work on Jill for a moment, and he went on at last.

"Then came a message, for me personally, from Donovan, a very frantic message. It seems that Ferret *did* drop, somewhere or other, and just disappeared, didn't even radio his safe arrival. The pilot, however, reported a perfect operation, he said he was right over the letters of the day..."

"Even though the fires were not burning properly?"

"Exactly. He said he saw the parachute open, he took off, and landed in England with nothing more than a few shrapnel holes in his fuselage."

There was a little silence, and then, "It stinks," Josh Dekker said. Hugh Black, listening, murmured, "I know what you're thinking, but don't jump to conclusions, Josh. There's not a pilot in the Air Force who's going to admit that he screwed up the operation if it had, in his opinion, a reasonable chance of success. What? He's going to say, 'Sorry, fellows, I dropped him fifteen miles off pinpoint?' It's not likely."

"We'll never know what happened," Lievre said wearily. "The pilot might easily have thought, quite genuinely, that he'd done the right thing. It was a bad night for a drop, he could have been killed."

"In which case," Josh said swiftly, "wouldn't you have heard about it?"

"Possibly."

Lievre was a little ill at ease, but he went on. "I put thirty men on it at once. We have our own people, as you know, in most of the Gestapo buildings in Paris itself, and all they could find out was that...well, he's not in any of them. So if he was captured...then where the hell is he?"

Del Adam sauntered over to them and sat down on the hard rock floor of the cave. "If this guy," he said, "is as important as Donovan believes, and if they really captured him on the drop, then isn't it possible that they've taken him to Germany? Wouldn't that be the sensible thing to do?"

Dekker nodded. "Yes, it's a possibility. But I don't think that's what happened." There was an echo of those voices in his mind. *They gave me forty-eight hours of duty in Marlotte jail, and I saw this guy... Christ, they had him trussed up like a turkey...*

He said slowly: "Tell me, Lievre, it's important. How many agents have been dropped to you in these past few weeks?"

"Just the one," Lievre said, "only Ferret, in the last, what, two months and a half."

"And is it possible that one from...from England, perhaps, could have parachuted in without your knowledge?"

"No, absolutely not. And they *all* come from England, British or American, the nearest airfields the allies have."

"Maybe somebody kind of sneaking in, and you not informed?"

Lievre was losing his very short patience. "Allied Intelligence is getting to be highly coordinated these days," he said emphatically. "In this area, there's not an allied agent *farts* without my knowledge. And that includes you, Josh Dekker."

"Then I know where he is," Dekker said. "He's in Marlotte jail, being given the electrical treatment. One wire down his throat, the other fastened to his genitals. We overheard a conversation"

"Then he'll be dead already," Lievre said instantly, "That method doesn't take very long. And his corpse will be thanking God that he is dead, believe me."

"Little bursts of current, switched on and off, not enough at a time to kill him."

"Then we can only pray that the man at the switch overdoes it, and puts him out of his anguish."

"They're experts in the Gestapo, they'll know just how far they can go and still keep him alive."

"Yes, I'm afraid you're right."

"And knowing where he is is half the battle, isn't it?"

"Yes. The easy half," Lievre said. "Getting him out of there borders on the impossible."

"Just tell my why."

"Because I know nothing at all about Marlotte jail." He shrugged. "I didn't even know that the Gestapo were using it."

"Can you infiltrate someone in there? Bearing in mind the fact that every five minutes this poor bastard is being kept alive he's suffering inconceivable agony?"

"I can, and I will. Marlotte is a very small town, and it has a strange reputation. For every fifty inhabitants, there are fifty-one patriots. I know what has to be done."

He sent for Roland, and said to him, "Take your bicycle and hurry to Marlotte. By this time tomorrow night, I want one of our people in the prison there, a servant. It will be best, perhaps, if it's a woman, but not a woman of immaculate chastity, you understand? She must be prepared for...for the inevitable."

"I understand."

Roland was indeed an understanding sort of man, in spite of his brutish appearance. "But I have only until tomorrow night? Better if you give me a week."

"Twenty-four hours," Lievre said, "no more. And a man's life hangs on it."

Marlotte was only an hour distant by bicycle, and it was nearly three o'clock in the morning when Roland knocked hesitantly at the door of a small house he knew.

It seemed an interminable time before his knock was answered. But then a small voice said from beyond the safety of a heavy timber door, "Yes? Who is it?"

"Roland, *mon petit*."

"Ah, Roland... Are you alone?"

"Just me, and my bicycle."

"Good."

There was the sound of innumerable bolts being thrown, and then the young girl was there, pulling open the door.

"Come in," she said, "quickly." She closed the door behind him, locked and counter-locked it again, and led him to the living room, lit by a solitary candle.

She grimaced. "That air raid knocked out the electricity."

He held up the bottle of wine he had brought with him, and grinned. "It's cold, I had it in my saddlebag wrapped up in a wet cloth."

She glanced at the grandfather clock in the corner; it was a few minutes after three o'clock. "But what is it that brings you visiting at three in the morning? There's a curfew here, didn't you know that? You can be shot on sight for breaking it."

"I know it. But I heard you were out of a job now."

She sighed. "The factory was almost completely demolished, that was quite an air raid, wasn't it? We all got laid off till it can get operating again; it might be months."

"Have you tried looking for work?"

"Half the population here is out of work."

"Have you tried the Germans?"

She flared. "Roland! How can you suggest such a thing! I hate the *Bosches!*"

He said gravely, "As any honest woman should. But all of Marlotie is against them, and it means that they can't find anyone to work for them."

"And that is exactly as it should be. *Mon Dieu*, Roland! You of all people ought to know this! Isn't that what the Resistance is all about?"

"No. We are no longer thinking in terms of *passive* resistance. We're striking out now into the very heart of German territory, placing our people in their headquarters, wherever we can. And right now...we need someone, very urgently, in the local jail. There's an American agent being held there. Lievre and his friend Josh Dekker are going to rescue him, if they can, before he dies under extreme torture. Before, if possible, he spills all the secrets he might be carrying in his mind. And every hour counts."

Her eyes were wide as he told her what was expected of her, and he said roughly, "You're not a virgin, it won't be too hard for you. A man inside you is a man, after all."

She whispered: "Not if he's German." But she looked him straight in the eye and said deliberately: "Very well. If it serves the Resistance, I will do what you ask."

"Not what I *ask*," Roland said. "But what we *demand*."

"To make a whore of me?"

"A very small step," Roland said dryly, "in the direction you've chosen to take for some time now. Drink up."

He raised his glass to hers, and as they drank together he told her exactly what had to be done.

"First, we need a good chart of the whole building, and the number of German troops there on any given day. Just who feeds the prisoners in the cellar? How many French are employed there, and to what extent can we count on them in an emergency? How many of them are Fascists, how many might be Communists working for themselves?"

The bottle was finished before he was through briefing her, and Roland said at last, majestically: "I will sleep the rest of the night here. All I need is six feet of floor space, and a blanket."

She brought him a comforter, and she whispered: "If you'd rather sleep with me, Roland, I don't mind. Honestly I don't."

He was very stern, a devoted husband, and the father of three delightful children.

"No," he said, "save yourself for the commanding officer of the jail. His name is Haugwitz, Captain Otto von Haugwitz. And we'll need your report...yesterday."

She hesitated. "And...do I get paid?"

Roland shook his head. "No, you don't. If they find you out, and you get to be killed off, we give your parents a little money. It's the custom."

She went to bed, and lay awake tossing and turning all might as she wondered what it was going to be like.

* * *

Her name was Monique Damas, and she was twenty-seven years old. She was not a raving beauty, but she was quite attractive, tall and slender, with a very good bust and nicely rounded hips and very well-formed legs. Her eyes were large and somewhat melancholy, her nose very aristocratic (no one quite knew how this had come about), and a wide forehead suggested a high degree of intelligence she didn't really enjoy.

But she was nice, a charming, outgoing young woman who was much younger than her true years; she thought, and lived, like a teenager.

And at nine o'clock in the morning, having cooked breakfast for Roland, she presented herself at Marlotte jail.

The Sergeant was bored, and Monique's unexpected appearance livened him up considerably. All the Gestapo personnel had been ordered into crash courses in French, and he laid down his book and said, in labored French, "Er, what can I do for you, Mad'moiselle?"

"I'm looking for work, Sergeant, and I want to talk with the Herr Hauptmann Haugwitz."

"If it's work you want... I can perhaps arrange it for you. In exchange for certain favors."

"The Herr *Hauptmann* is a personal friend, Sergeant."

"Oh." He was terribly alarmed. "Well, in that case, chère Mad'moiselle, I excuse myself. May I know your name?"

"I am Monigue Damas."

"Monique Damas. Yes. Excuse me."

He went to the inner room and said to the officer there, "There's a French woman to see you, Sir. She says she knows you."

Captain Haugwitz looked up from the papers he was studying, and said, "Her name?"

"Monique Damas, Herr *Hauptmann*."

"I never even heard of her. Well, show her in."

She was dressed very modestly in a high-buttoned blouse and a medium-length skirt as she stood before him. He said, sarcastically, his feet up on the desk, "Monique Damas, a friend of mine. But this is the

35

first occasion on which I have even heard your name."

He was blond and blue eyed, very Aryan and quite handsome, and he said, "I wonder why it is that you choose these deceptions to meet with me?"

"Because," Monique said calmly, "I do not like to deal with sergeants and corporals."

"Oh?" His eyes were on her, he asked, "Does that mean to say that you consider yourself officer material?"

"Yes. I am officer material."

"And you're looking for a job? What? Scrubbing floors? Cleaning out toilets? Waiting on tables?"

"All or any of those things. I just need a paid job, a weekly wage. I honestly don't care what it is."

That little silence. Then, the captain said softly, "You realize that all the townspeople of Marlotte will ostracize you?"

"And while they starve to death, I will be paid enough to eat well, I hope. I am a survivor. I will do anything I must to *survive*." She said again, pointedly, "Anything at all."

"I am glad to hear it. Your duties would be those of a servant, of course. But there would be other obligations, too."

Monique dropped her eyes, hoping it gave the appearance of shyness, and she whispered, "I will do whatever is required of me, Sir, I promise."

"Good. Take off your clothes."

"In...in here?" She stammered: "Someone might come, Herr *Hauptmann*."

"Do as you're told," the Captain said wearily. "I will not hire you if your breasts hang down to your damned knees, it's as simple as that. So be quick about it. I want to see your naked body."

"Well, if you're sure."

"The blouse first, and then the skirt." He was giggling now, like a foolish schoolboy. "Then the bra, and the panties."

Monique did as she was told, and stood before him as bare as the day she was born, her hands modestly masking the pubic area.

"Your hands behind your back," he said, and when she obeyed him he undid the buttons of his fly and began playing with himself till the tension became unbearable.

36

And then, "On your knees," he said. "You know what you have to do now, so do it. And do it well, if you want a job."

She obeyed him again, and it was not too hard for her; the Captain was a very *good-looking* young man, and this was nothing new for her; she did not even have to remind herself that it was all for a good cause.

But then, he made her put her blouse and skirt back on and just sit there in a corner while he went on with his work.

And twice in the course of the next three hours, he had her bend over his desk and sodomized her, quite ignoring her plaintive cries for vaseline to make it less painful for her.

And in the middle of the afternoon, fully satiated now, he said to her roughly, "You will report to Sergeant Wagner in the kitchen, in charge of the officers' mess. And if he tries to force his attentions on you, as he well might, you will refuse him, is that understood?"

"Understood, Herr *Hauptmann*," Monique said meekly.

"You are indeed officer material. You will not spread your legs for the lower ranks. There is one other captain in this establishment, and five lieutenants. You will make yourself available to all of us, on demand, for whatever is demanded of you, is that clear?"

"Clear, Herr *Hauptmann*."

"Good. So go now. There will be pots that require scrubbing."

Sergeant Wagner turned out to be an uncouth and brutal man who had failed officer class three times in a row. He was thickset, squat, and very muscular, with beetle brows and hardly any forehead at all; he had a dreadful chip on his shoulder.

He said to her: "Monique? That's a good French name, and I like the French women, they're terrific. And all you have to do is understand that in this kitchen *I'm* the boss, what I say goes, whether you like it or not. And if you like it, so much the better, we'll get along just fine."

He found a white sheet and spread it quickly over the long butcher-block table where the meat for the officers' mess was carved up, and he patted it and said, "Come on, what are you waiting for? Up! On your back, and spread your legs."

Monique sighed, and once again did as she was told. The Sergeant unbuttoned his fly and spread himself clumsily over her, and fumbled at her skirt and her panties, and drove himself into her furiously with no benefit of foreplay at all, in full view of all the kitchen help.

It was merely a matter of the territorial imperative.

Eighteen hours later, Roland bicycled by the jail and picked up a note that had been left, by prearrangement, under bomb-shattered bricks in the jail's wail. There were five pages, closely written in a small and quite childish handwriting.

'Two captains, five Lieutenants, fourteen non-commissioned officers, with 240 to 270 troopers, almost all of them from the Seventh Parachute Battalion. The top floor of this three-story building is given over to the officers' sleeping quarters, the second floor is the housing for the troops, the ground floor contains the administrative offices, and in the cellar, consisting of seven underground rooms, there were, until this morning, eighty-four French hostages being held, men, women, and children. But this morning, at five o clock, thirty of them were driven to Paris for public execution in retaliation for the killing of a German officer on the Champs Elysées the other night. There is also an American spy in the cellar. So far, even after all this time, it seems that they have not broken him.'

There was a great deal more, and Roland murmured, as he bicycled off to the safe-house and Lievre, "God bless you, poor Monique."

And less than an hour later, Josh Dekker, Lievre, Del Adams, Ira Watslaw, and Mike Homer were squatting in a circle in the hideout cave, studying Monique's report. Hugh Black, a little apart from them, was kneeling beside a sleeping Jill Magran, still worrying about her.

Josh Dekker said, "Lievre, can we get a diversion when we need it, from your fellows?"

"I'll take care of it," Lievre answered promptly.

"I'll take a hundred and fifty men or so and fake an attack on their armory. It'll draw most of the troops out of the jail, for sure. Armed with machine pistols and grenades, we'll sound like an army of a thousand."

"Great. How far is the jail from the armory?"

"A mile and a half, I think. Not much more, anyway."

"It couldn't be more perfect. Okay." He looked around at the others. "Ira, tomorrow night?"

"Any time you say, Josh."

"Okay. I need..." He got to his feet and went over to look down at Jill, sleeping there like a child, and he said gently, "Will you stay with her, Hugh? An attack on this safe-house is always possible. She can't take care of herself now, I'd like to be sure that. "

The British ex-Major interrupted him. "I love her maybe even more than you do, Josh, won't you ever understand that? *Nothing* is going to happen to her while I'm still alive. And I have to remind you, at this point, that I don't die easily."

"Okay. Ira, you in your Gestapo colonel's uniform, to do all the talking. Del, you and Mike as rude and licentious German soldiery. And I'll be the Sergeant."

"Why," Mike Homer asked plaintively, "why can't *I*, just once in a while, be the Sergeant? If not an officer?"

"We'll need a German vehicle of some sort," Josh Dekker said. "That's your assignment for the moment. Find us one, preferably with Gestapo license plates, and have it ready for us."

"Okay, you got it."

For more than two hours, they discussed the intricacies of this operation.

Three hours later they were ready to go.

CHAPTER 4

The rescue of Lieutenant Miles Foresome, code-named Ferret, was a classic operation; like all classic operations, it was carried out with dispatch and the highest efficiency, and in no time at all.

At H-Hour, which happened to be shortly after ten o'clock in the evening, the moon just sinking, Lievre's 152 men opened a simulated attack on the Marlotte Armory, keeping their distance and not looking for a fight against impossible odds.

Some two hundred of the troops stationed in the Marlotte jail turned out to join their coworkers at the armory, leaving the jail very vulnerable indeed, and they were quickly reinforced by another eight hundred plus who descended with commendable speed on the scene of what looked like a major battle.

Were upon, Lievre's men began a slow and calculated withdrawal.

But meanwhile...

It took Del Adam two minutes to send the anchors, with Hugh Black's little cross bow, up to the roof of the jail, another three minutes to swarm up its rope, and five more to place the *plastique* explosives where they would do the most damage.

And only thirty seconds after he had rappelled down to the alleyway, the top of the building simply disintegrated in a massive explosion that shook almost half the town.

They were crouched very close to the walls of the building, sheltering themselves from the falling concrete as best they could.

And when the last of the rubble had fallen Josh Dekker said tightly, "All right, let's go."

* * *

From now on, it was a matter of one-two-three.

They broke down the rear door of the building, and strode into it—a Gestapo colonel (a Polish Jew from Warsaw) accompanied by his sergeant bodyguard, whose name was Josh Dekker (an American parachutist from the legendary Hundred and First), with two Gestapo soldiers marching alongside them, Del Adam (a blade-man from Lebanon), and Mike Homer (an American flyer who was quite ready to throw his life away at the drop of a hat—provided it would help defeat the Germans).

In no time at all, they found the woman named Monique, warned in advance by Roland and therefore looking for them too.

She led them in the chaos to the cellars, and everywhere they moved there were panic-stricken German soldiers, some of them so scared that they even forgot about saluting Ira Watslaw's uniform.

The whole building was beginning to collapse now with the weight of the shattered concrete up there.

They found the wreck of the man code-named Ferret, and he was naked as the day he was born, with the deep marks, down to the bone, of the whip at his back; the area around the top of his thighs was blackened where it had been slowly burned.

Ira Watslaw said sharply to the three frightened guards there, "Cut him loose! We are taking him to a safer place."

There was a certain amount of the Heil Hitler crap as a knife appeared to slice through the ropes at his ankles and his wrists, and then the prisoner was free. Dreadfully unsteady on his feet, he looked at Ira Watslaw's Gestapo Colonel and suddenly spat in his face, and he said, his voice weak but filled with venom, "Just to show you what I think of the goddamn Gestapo, pig..."

But Del Adam, for reasons of his own, had slipped his favorite blade into his hand, and he suddenly shouted: "Hi, hi, hi!" And with each *Hi!* he had slashed open a German throat.

There were three dead bodies on the ground, and the room was now theirs.

Josh Dekker said to Ferret, very quietly, "We're working at the moment at least, for Donovan in Cairo. And the object of this exercise is to get you the hell out of here. Can you walk?"

"You better believe it. If it has to kill me, I can walk."

"Okay, you're our prisoner, we're taking you to a safer place, someone knocked the top two stories off this building."

"I got it."

Automatically, he held out his wrists for Dekker to bind them, and Dekker murmured, "Looks to me like you're one tough sonofabitch. You think you can make it?"

"If you can, then I can too."

"Then let's go."

The prisoner was dead on his feet, but supporting himself by sheer willpower, a man to be reckoned with. He said, hesitantly, looking at Ira Watslaw, "Just keep that fucking Gestapo Colonel out of my hair, or I'm liable to kill him."

"That fucking Gestapo Colonel," Dekker said mildly, "happens to be a Polish prick from Warsaw. He's on our side, don't worry about it; we couldn't have gotten near you without him."

"Okay, I can live with that."

But suddenly, this strong man rolled up his eyes and collapsed. Del Adam caught him before he hit the ground.

"It had to catch up with him sooner or later," he said. "I don't care how tough he likes to think he is. The human body can only stand so much. But we've got a good man on our hands. I think."

It was midnight in the candlelit cave, and the doctor was still there.

He threw up his hands as he bent over Ferret's unconscious body, and he said helplessly, "What, you expect me to bring a dead man back to life? No, I cannot, it is beyond my capabilities. I give this wreck of what was once a man another few hours before his poor heart stops beating. What we have here is a case of auricular fibrillation; his body has suffered more than his heart can tolerate."

"Digitalis," Hugh Black said tightly. "Do you have it?"

"No, I do not." The old doctor looked at him strangely. "Are you a medical man, Sir?"

Hugh shook his head. "No, I cannot claim that honor."

42

"And yet you know, and I will instantly agree with you, that the only medication that might perhaps save this poor fellow's life is digitalis. Which we do not have."

"I was once trained," Hugh Black said tightly, "in the art of survival. And in a forest..."

He turned to an anxious Lievre, and said, "Foxgloves. Surely in a forest like this, there must be foxgloves growing?"

Bewildered, Lievre nodded. "Of course. By the thousand, everywhere. It's a weed here."

"Then send someone, quickly, to bring us a dozen plants or so. Just root them up, we need the leaves."

"I know just where to find them," Roland said, and he was gone instantly.

And now, there began an earnest conversation between a doctor with ages-old training, and an upstart who had learned, in his survival courses, about herbs and their medical importance.

The old doctor said, "We can't extract the oil, it will take far too long, and we'd need a dozen bushels."

Hugh Black answered, "No, we don't even need that. We make a strong infusion, a kind of tea."

"It has to be very, very strong."

"Yes. I'm sure of it. So let's *make* it strong. Two or three handfuls of leaves to a pint of boiling water; let's infuse it for ten minutes at least. It's very simply a question of getting digitalis into his system, one way or another."

The old doctor looked at him curiously. "Will you tell me where you discovered that the foxglove is the major source of digitalis? It's not commonly known to the ordinary layman."

Hugh Black sighed. "Can you believe," he said, "that at my great age I was trained as a commando? They taught me these things, how to survive in a jungle or a forest without the benefit of medical supplies or food. Then, they discovered that my limbs were too fragile for jumping out of aircraft, so I was quietly transferred to Intelligence, and I loved every minute of it. But..."

He was laughing softly. "But one night I got smashed, and I paid off all my tabs in the Birka, that's Cairo's major brothel area, with rubber checks. So, I was cashiered. It was the end of my military career and of my marriage too. When Josh Dekker found me, I was holding down the only job I could find. I was keeping the books in a whorehouse."

Roland returned, panting, and the water was already boiling on the thorn-twig fire. They made the tea with the foxglove leaves, pure digitalis, and they fed it to the man who was close to death.

And within the hour, he was beginning his return to the land of the living.

Jill, too, was recovering.

With Josh Dekker and the others, she sat on the hard earth floor of the cave while Roland served them a brace of rabbits he had caught in his traps, with a salad of dandelion leaves, a little bitter because he had not been able to blanch them properly.

The man code-named Ferret was very weak indeed, and Josh Dekker knew instinctively that this was the best possible time to question him.

"Will you tell me your real name? I'm Josh Dekker."

"Yes, I know, Donovan told me all about you. He says you're a number one sonofabitch, that you don't work for him anymore, he's cut you off from...from financing, supplies, from everything. Is it true?"

"It's true. We don't even exchange insults any more. I screwed up on a job he gave me to do. I was supposed to bring out a leader of the Resistance named Catinat. We got him out of prison, an operation just like this one. Only, Lievre here knocked him off, and Donovan didn't like that too much."

Lievre said stolidly, "I did what had to be done." Josh Dekker said instantly, "He's right. Given the same circumstances, I would have done the same thing."

"Thank you, Josh Dekker," Lievre said sourly. "You never told me that before."

"I never had occasion to."

He turned back to Ferret. "You were going to tell me your name."

"Oh, was I?"

Dekker said patiently, "We'll have to find out if the Germans know it, so don't be so fucking coy."

There was a long, deep sigh; and then, "Well, okay, my name is Foresome, Miles Foresome. Donovan gave me the codename Ferret."

He was desperately weak, a good time to solve some of the problems that were bugging the hell out of Dekker.

So Dekker said carefully, "Tell me what it is so special about you, Miles Foreman?"

"Special about me? Why, nothing."

"*Balls*. Donovan's message about you had panic, pure *panic*, in every phrase. And it's out of character for him. Donovan sends people like you and me to their deaths every day of his fucking life, and he doesn't give a shit about it. But hey, suddenly there's an agent named Ferret he's really worried about. Tell me *why*, Miles Foresome."

There was a long, long silence; it seemed to Dekker that Miles Foresome had suddenly awoken to some kind of danger he was in.

But then he said, very slowly, "I was carrying a suitcase, Dekker. It contains the name of every single agent Donovan has in France, yours included." He shrugged. "Well, I guess your name doesn't matter that much, the Gestapo already knows it, from way back. But all the others—most of them are very, very secret."

Josh Dekker felt the hair rising at the back of his scalp. "And where is this suitcase now?"

"I hid it, stashed it away before they captured me. And in case you're worrying about it, I told them *nothing*. Why do you think I'm still alive? Because they were still *trying*."

And now, out came all the bitterness. "I'm only half a man, Dekker." The voice was harsh. "They burned my cock and my balls down to the bone. I'll never be able to fuck again as long as I live."

He touched his forehead. "But this—my *mind*, Dekker, it's still a good mind in spite of the torture. They destroyed me physically, but they left a brain. You see, they made a mistake."

Josh Dekker sighed. "Before we go any further," he said, "I want to know a great deal more about you. First of all—nationality?"

Was there a hesitation?

"American," Miles Foresome said.

"I detect a touch of a foreign accent, and I'm not good with them. Is it German?"

"I was born and bred in Switzerland. I'm an American citizen now."

"But you speak fluent German?"

"Naturally. My home town was once Zurich. Now, it's San Francisco. But I'm an engineer, I was working in Cairo when Colonel Donovan found me, building pontoon bridges for the canal."

Josh' Dekker turned to Ira Watslaw, the linguist. "Take over, Ira. You know what it is I want to find out."

Ira said, in German, *"Wo haben Sie Englisch gelernt?"* He was asking where Foresome had learned his English.

And now, there was a long and careful conversation in German. It seemed that Ferret was fast recovering, though his voice was hoarse, coming through with the greatest difficulty.

"I was born in Switzerland, as I told you. I went to good schools, where we learned, apart from our native German, English, French, and Italian. I immigrated to America twelve years ago, and have been an American citizen for the last five years."

"Tell me about this suitcase you were carrying. Containing the names of all the OSS agents in France, you say. This sounds to me like a very grave breach of security. How could Donovan permit such a thing? He's not a fool."

Ferret had the grace to seem embarrassed. "There were one hundred and seventeen names. I was supposed to memorize them." He grimaced. "For once, I overestimated my abilities. I failed to memorize the names quickly. I will admit, I should have destroyed the list, I did not."

"You don't need a suitcase for a couple of pages of paper. What else does it contain?"

There was no hesitation at all this time. "My radio equipment."

"And where, precisely, did you hide it?"

"High up in a tree in the forest, just outside a place called Marlotte."

"Could you find it again if we took you there?"

"Yes, of course. And that is something we have to do, quite

urgently. It's really very compromising."

"Yes, so you said."

Ira Watslaw, an expert linguist, switched easily to Italian. "*E parli anche Italiano, n'e vero*? You speak Italian too?"

"*Ma si, sicuro*. Yes, of course."

They talked in Italian for a while, and then in French for a long time more. And Ira Watslaw said at last, in English, "He's okay, Josh. He's perfect Donovan material."

"Well, thank God for that."

Ira looked at his watch. "And I have to check on the sentries, I didn't realize how late it was."

"Yes, of course."

Check on the sentries? Ira?

It was hardly Ira's responsibility. Josh Dekker looked at Lievre and saw no expression on his face at all. He said, smiling, "Maybe I should come with you, stretch my legs. Caves get to be a little claustrophobic, don't they?"

He followed Ira out, and in a little while, when they were far out of earshot of the cave, Josh was suddenly aware that Lievre, unaccountably furious, was hurrying to catch up to them.

Dekker said to Ira, "Okay, what the hell's the fuss about?"

Ira did not answer him. Instead, he turned to Lievre. "How much of that did you understand?"

"All of the English," Lievre answered, "all of the French, naturally, almost all of the German, and a little of the Italian. And that man is lying through his teeth."

Ira nodded. "Yes. And I'm glad you agree with me."

He turned to Josh, and he said quietly, "Josh, you're at a disadvantage here, because of linguistics. That Ferret comes off okay, maybe, in English and in German too, his mother tongue. But in Italian, he's just too damned smooth."

"And in French too," Lievre said, and the Pole nodded. "Yes, his languages are immaculate, almost as good as mine. But—did you know this? In a language that isn't naturally your own, you can give yourself away so very easily. It's what?" He turned to Lievre. "His choice of words?"

"*Phraseology*," Lievre said. "What he had to say in French.

47

Yes, you found the right word exactly. It was all too *smooth*."

Ira turned back to Josh Dekker. "Nothing you can put your finger on," he said. "But yes, he's just too damned plausible. But, I might be very wrong, of course."

Josh thought about it for a moment or two, and he said at last, very quietly, "Are you suggesting that we've had an agent foisted on us? Is that what we're faced with?"

Ira Watslaw shook his head. "No," he said emphatically. "That man's been beaten, very cruelly. Those stripes on his back are down to the bone. I don't think that even the Gestapo could persuade a man to suffer like this to make a point. And you saw what happened to his balls?"

"Well, we have to admit that this is a very tough sonofabitch. I still don't believe it." Josh Dekker turned to Lievre. "Can we get the doctor in on this discussion?"

Lievre nodded. "I'll get him."

It was merely a question of verification, but when the old medic appeared, Josh Dekker said slowly, "A foolish question, perhaps. But tell me, how badly has this man been hurt?"

"Beyond the point of survival," the doctor said at once. "He should be dead. The burning of his genitals would have killed an ordinary man, but there's worse, far worse. The inside of his mouth is burned, his throat, you heard how he talks. And I'm surprised, in view of the damage, that he can even articulate a single syllable. And there's still worse. God alone knows what his insides are like, I'd need to operate to determine that. And yet he's still *compus mentis*, surviving by willpower and nothing else! This is a very strong man, Mr. Dekker. He's struggling to stay alive! Perhaps he can win that battle, perhaps not, I just don't know."

The old man, out of his depth, was searching for the words, and finding them only with the greatest difficulty.

He said at last, very hesitantly, "I am a medical doctor, Mr. Dekker. That is to say, I am only concerned with *bodily* ills. I know very little about their effect on the mind; this is an entirely different area of medicine. And all I can tell you is that this man, for reasons of his own, is driving himself to the very limits of perseverance and...and of determination. There's something he just *has* to live for."

He threw up his hands in an eloquent gesture. "I have no idea what it might be."

The other invalid, Jill Magran, was recovering faster; she, too, was strong on determination.

They had all moved out of the stifling atmosphere of the cave, into the warm summer forest itself for the night, Jill and Josh Dekker were close beside each other in their respective sleeping bags, with Hugh Black; Ira Watslaw, Del Adam, and Mike Homer under their own chosen bushes not too far away. The doctor was staying over, convinced that his services would soon be needed again, and was sleeping in the cave with his charge Ferret, with Lievre and a dozen of his men stretched out on the floor, their guns and grenades ready beside them.

And the woods were filled with the men of the Resistance. For the moment, at least, this was a very safe place to be.

There had been great activity all through the day, no less than seven fire companies from Paris at work on the forest fire, finally bringing it under control toward midnight.

And as far as the Paris fire department was concerned, the Germans just didn't trust them. They believed (quite correctly) that there were far too many patriots among them.

It meant that for a full day and half a night, the whole of the immediate area was ringed with German troops, on the lookout for a band of freebooter American commandoes who seemed to have escaped the trap that had been inexorably closing around them.

But for the time being, at least, Josh Dekker and his group—in the Germans' midst—were safe.

It was Jill's idea that Dekker leave his own sleeping bag and join her in hers, half unzipped now to accommodate both naked bodies. He worried about her condition, worried about ripping the good doctor's expert stitches. But she insisted, and he gave way to her, as he always did in the end.

Very gently, he settled himself half behind her, parted her thighs to accept him, and carefully eased himself into her. He was very excited, and he came far more quickly than he had intended. But he stayed contained within her, and he whispered, "The next time will be better for you, my darling."

"It was good this time too."

"Yes, I know it. And why don't you sleep for a while?"

"All right. But asleep or awake, I want to feel you still there."

"I will be."

In between bouts of lovemaking, he told her of the operation, of the rescue of a man code-named Ferret.

"It was perfect," he said, "it went absolutely according to plan, even down to the timing. We brought it in seven minutes under schedule, with no casualties at all."

"I'm only sorry I wasn't there. For the next one, I promise you I will be."

"Our next will be the recovery of Ferret's famous suitcase."

She was puzzled, but only a little. "But...surely, you know where it is?"

"Yes. It's in the upper branches of an ancient oak tree, standing somewhere at the western extremity of the Gorge aux Loups, the Valley of the Wolves."

"Then...isn't it merely a question of sending someone there to retrieve it? With or without Ferret? That's hardly an *operation*."

"Wouldn't it be wonderful if it were as simple as that?"

Her eyes were wide in the darkness. "But, it's not?"

Josh Dekker said deliberately, "One tree among twenty or thirty at the western extremity of the gorge, it will take a little finding, even if Ferret can lead us to it. He may not be able to; that man's closer to death now than to life."

"But I still don't see the difficulty." Sarcastically, she added, "Tell me roughly where it is, and I'll go fetch it for you."

He sighed. "Only one problem, my sweet."

"And what is that?"

"We have to find that suitcase before someone just stumbles onto it."

"Of course! But even so..."

"And Lievre tells me," Josh Dekker said, "that for the last five days and nights, the Germans have been building a weapons and ammunitions dump at that precise location. It's also going to house the administrative offices of the Paris Gestapo, Southern Urban Division."

"Oh God."

"It means that as of this moment, Ferret's suitcase is hidden in the upper branches of an oak tree right in the middle of a fucking German camp. And to make room for their buildings, the Nazis are beginning to cut down the oaks. It's only a question of time before they find it."

CHAPTER 5

The man called Ferret was one of the toughest survivors in history. The old doctor could only shake his head in wonder, and murmur, "When you brought him to me, I was sure he would not last for more than a few hours. But he seems to be recovering. His speech is coming back, the burns in his mouth are healing faster than I would have thought possible. His genitals? No, they'll never function again. And the damage that's been done to what's inside that poor body— only God or a first-rate surgeon can tell us, and I'm neither. There is only one solution, my friends, to this pressing problem. And that is to send him to England for treatment that might save his life. Without which, he's liable to die at any moment."

He took off his thick-lensed glasses and wiped at them with a gray pocket handkerchief that had once been virgin white.

"It's none of my business, of course, I realize that. But they do tell me that light planes from England can land here once in a while, for missions just like this. It's the only way to ensure his survival, gentlemen."

Josh Dekker went to the cave and made the proposition to Ferret who was lying on his mattress, deathly white and in obvious pain. But he seemed mentally alert, and listened patiently to the suggestion. In a display of sheer will, he forced himself to his feet and stood there, not even swaying. He said calmly, "I came here on a mission of the utmost importance, Dekker, a mission I intend to complete, so don't make like my nursemaid, I don't need one. And my only problem at the moment is—how you found out about me."

"Donovan told me," Dekker said. Was there a moment of

alarm on that ravaged face?

No, it quickly changed to an expression of disbelief, and Ferret said dryly, "Colonel Donovan told me that you were no longer working for him, that he'd fired you. He said you're not even in radio contact."

"He didn't fire me," Dekker said patiently, "I opted out. I screwed up on a mission. Donovan wanted me back in Cairo for an enquiry, possibly for a court-martial, so I told him politely to go fuck himself. Ever since, we've been operating as freebooters, just helping to win this goddamn war the way we see fit. It's a great life."

"And he told you about me?" Those intelligent eyes were probing, full of suspicion.

"Through Lievre. He couldn't help, and by sheer luck, I could. That's the story in a nutshell."

"Are you still in touch with Donovan?"

"No way. As far as I'm concerned, he can go to hell. And did you hear what's probably happening to your secret oak tree? The Jerries may be chopping it down right now. They're building themselves a fucking great camp in the gorge, and cutting down trees to make room for it. Your tree might even be laid horizontal by now, in which case, we're dead. And you're going to have to come with us, I'm afraid, to identify it. I don't want any men climbing twenty or thirty trees in the hope of finding the right one. Are you up to it?"

"*Up to it?*" Ferret echoed. "Of course I am! What's more, I'll take over the whole operation for you, just give me twenty good men—"

"No, you will not," Dekker said. "All you will do is point a finger and say, *That one*. And the rest is up to me."

"Okay, I accept. And the operation is when?"

"Friday night. The moon sets at ten-thirty. We go in at twenty-three hundred hours exactly, the six of us. At the eastern extremity of the gorge, which is only half a mile or so away, Lievre will be mounting a diversionary attack with four hundred men, to draw them away from where we'll be operating."

There was a little pause, and then, "You're sure you can make it? You look like hell to me."

"And I feel like hell," Ferret said tightly. "But I have a job to do, and I'm going to do it, so just don't bug me. Help me retrieve that suitcase, and I'll love you like a brother."

"That kind of gratitude I can do without."

"And I want to send a message to Donovan," Ferret said, "just to reassure him. I don't want to wait till we recover my suitcase and the radio in it. Can I use yours?"

"I'm not in direct radio contact with Donovan anymore, I think he told you that. It has to go through Lievre."

There was that awful silence again for a moment, and then Ferret said smoothly, "You and I both realize that it has to be top secret. Will Lievre send it blind? Not knowing what it says? Just one message, and then no more. The Resistance *must* not know what it says, Dekker."

"I don't like it."

"Like it or not, we're both OSS. And you and I both know that the Resistance is not always to be trusted. In this case, we must be one hundred percent sure. One single message, Dekker, before I recover my own radio."

Josh Dekker said, very offhandedly, "I'm sure I can persuade him. At least, I think I can. Let's all get together in the morning. Good night, Ferret."

Ferret went back to his mattress and rolled himself up in a blanket; Josh Dekker couldn't help wondering if he'd ever wake up again.

"No," Lievre said. "I will never allow a blind message sent over my radio. I want to know what it is that Ferret has to say to Donovan. If it's so top secret that I can't know about it—and in my territory, mark you—then it won't be sent over this radio."

"Do me this one favor," Josh Dekker said. "I promise you I'll find out what it's about, and as soon as I do...you will be told."

"Yes?" Lievre was almost snarling. "He's presumably using L.M.T., it's not a code that you can break very easily."

"Jill can break it."

"*L.M.T.?* It would take her six months."

"Three days, provided it's not too short."

"Are you serious?"

"Ask her. She's an expert. It's not easy, I admit, but give her time...three days, maybe a week. All I need is a copy of what you send."

"If I know this man, he'll be sitting right by any operator to make sure there are no copies."

"Once we have the message in our hands, we keep him away from the radio."

Lievre nodded. "Yes, of course. We can do that very easily, can't we? Very well then, I agree."

"Good."

And so it was settled.

Three hours later, Ferret, on his feet again, produced two slips of paper for Dekker and Lievre.

The first was a message in code, groups of five letters preceded by a three digit number. And a second.

Ferret said ruefully, "I had second thoughts about my request. I realized that you both had every reason to know just what it was I wanted to say to Donovan. So...here's the message in clear."

It read: FERRET TO DONOVAN DUE TO EFFORTS OF DEKKER AND LIEVRE AM BACK IN CIRCULATION AND CONTINUING MISSION STOP STRONGLY REPEAT STRONGLY. SUGGEST DEKKER BE BROUGHT BACK INTO ORGANIZATION STOP HE IS INVALUABLE MESSAGE ENDS.

As Josh Dekker read it and passed it silently to Lievre, Ferret said wryly, "I'm not really that nice a guy. But I reflected. You got me out of that Gestapo torture chamber, still alive, and I owe you. I *owe* you, Dekker! And this is the least I can do for you."

Dekker sighed. "Well, that's real nice of you. Except that, no way I'm ever going to work for Donovan again."

"*Funding*," Ferret said, urging. "Money being paid into your Cairo bank account every month. Supplies being dropped to you when you need them—food, weapons, ammunition."

"Money?" Dekker said. "We have a major bank robbery coming up very shortly, the banks in Paris are controlled by the Germans now, and we're going to be the best financed operation in history. Food? You want us to live on K-Rations? In Paris, for Christ's sake? Weapons and ammunition? We have our own supply source, and it's a very good one—the German Army."

He added, "But I thank you, nonetheless, for the thought."

Ferret grunted. "Well, let's send the message anyway, and the Colonel can do what he likes with it. He has to know that I'm functioning again, poor sonofabitch worries about me, it ruins his Turf Club dinners."

"I doubt very much that he worries about you, or anyone else. You and I, Ferret, we're all expendable. He just replaces us if we get to be horizontal under a couple of feet of earth. The Germans bury their victims very quickly, did you know that? They're concerned about the flies, they're sanitation oriented."

"Send the message," Ferret said.

And to everyone's surprise, he made no effort at all to sit there with the radio operator when the message was sent. Was it because he *knew* that his code could never be broken?

"And will you tell me," Lievre said gently, "just what your mission is?"

"Of course," Ferret said instantly, "you have every right to know! It's to evaluate the importance of the Resistance to the war effort. De Gaulle wants to know, Churchill wants to know, Eisenhower wants to know, too. And I'd have you know that I'm already impressed by its efficiency."

Lievre made no attempt to hide his sarcasm.

"Thank you so much," he said sourly.

Cairo was hot as hell, even in the shaded confines of the Garden City on the east bank of the River Nile.

But there was a comic kind of air-conditioning in Colonel Donovan's office, and as long as the electricity held out, it worked just fine.

His hard-boiled P.A., Vera Vallance, had purchased two damn

great blocks of ice, delivered that morning from the ice factory in Heliopolis, one for her room and one for his. Electric fans were playing over them and bringing the temperature down to a comfortable eighty-five or so. It was still early in the day, but the night had been impossibly humid.

She brought a message into the Colonel's office and said, with a kind of satisfaction in her voice, "Ferret, Colonel. We've heard from him at last, so it seems your message to Dekker paid off. At four o'clock this morning, Foustani got a radio contact, isn't that great?"

Ahmed Foustani was their top radio operator, a man who could tap the key at an unbelievable speed while munching on a sandwich, and never make a mistake. He was smart and devious, always smiling to show what a nice guy he was. He was twenty-eight years old, flamboyantly handsome, and liked to think of himself as a ladies' man, often bringing flowers from his little garden in Zamalek to place in the vase on Vera's desk.

He was also secretly working for the Germans and the Italians, a double agent, and moreover was not averse to taking money from anyone who would pay him—like Lievre, in Paris.

Surprisingly, though the Italian espionage network was well-established in Cairo at this time, the Germans had only one solitary agent still working here, the others having been removed by the British MI5 very shortly after the outbreak of the war, which for them was September, 1939. Only one of the many had escaped the net.

His name was Hans Frederik Schneider, and British Intelligence, somehow, did not even know of his existence. He lived on a *dahabiyah*, a sort of sailing houseboat, moored at Gezira Island in the middle of the Nile, right opposite the famous Gezira Club where, posing as a neutral Swiss businessman, he was very much at home.

And Ahmed Foustani, firmly established—and trusted—in Colonel Donovan's OSS Headquarters, was Hans Schneider's most important underling.

(Schneider, the espionage case against him beyond any doubt at all, was arrested on the tenth day of February, 1943, and taken to the British Military Barracks in Abbasia for questioning; some twelve hours later, the word was passed around that he had been shot to death while attempting to escape the custody of the MPs.)

But now, Vera Vallance held out the radio message to her boss and said, sighing, "That Josh Dekker! It seems he's determined to keep on giving us trouble."

She was in her early thirties, long legged and willowy, small in the waist and the ass, not so small up front, with the kind of firm breasts that any virile man looking at them wanted to nibble on.

In spite of a formidable sexual appearance she was known to be quite unapproachable, she seldom dated anyone even for dinner or lunch, and invariably slept in her own bed, alone. But when she played with herself, as she often did, the object of her fantasies was always that disreputable renegade Josh Dekker.

Donovan read the message aloud; it had nothing whatsoever to do with the message in clear that Ferret had given to Dekker.

FERRET TO DONOVAN DEKKER IS IN MY HAIR STOP GET HIM OFF MY BACK BY WHATEVER MEANS OR THIS MISSION WILL FAIL REPEAT FAIL STOP HE KNOWS NOTHING OF THIS MESSAGE STOP MONEY IS IN GREAT JEOPARDY NOW MESSAGE ENDS

"That sonofabitch Dekker," the Colonel said, exploding. "I should have terminated him a long time ago. I sometimes have this strange feeling that at heart I'm just a pussycat. I wonder what would happen if I told Lievre to knock him off?"

Vera shrugged. "We can't even guess at that, can we? We don't know how well or how badly Dekker gets along with the Resistance. The fact that he's lasted this long would indicate, to me at east, that he and Lievre are probably buddy-buddy by now. And if that should be true, an order like that would lose us Group 47 altogether."

"Well," Wild Bill said, grumbling, "if Ferret pulls off his mission, we'll lose them anyway."

She agreed at once. "But," she said, "we don't want them to know that. Not yet."

She was right, of course and the Colonel knew it. "And I never saw a more ridiculous message in my whole life! Here we have a man disappearing for a week or more, no one knows what happened to him, and all he can say is, *Dekker's not being nice to me*. I don't like it,

V.V.! Why is he still with Dekker after all this time, instead of where he's supposed to be? I've a very nasty feeling that we're being screwed, expertly. Find out from Foustani if he recognized the hand of whoever sent this message."

"It was one of Lievre's operators," she said at once, and the Colonel glared at her. "Can he be sure of that? I know Foustani's good, but—"

"He's damned good," Vera said, interrupting him. "Lievre has five operators, and Foustani can recognize the touch of every one of them, with absolute assurance. There's nothing strange about that, any competent operator can do it. He just does it faster, and with more certainty. It was the one he calls Lievre's Number Three."

"Then I say again," Donovan declared wrathfully, "what in hell is Ferret doing still chumming around with Lievre and Dekker? He was scheduled to leave them within two hours of what we know was a very successful drop. Something went wrong, and by God, I have a right to know what it was!"

He calmed down a little, and half mumbled, "It's my own damned fault, I should have delayed the operation for a week or ten days and given Ferret a quick course in radio. I damn nearly did..."

"You can't turn out a radio operator in less than four or five months, not if he's going to be any good, you know that. Besides, there was no reason to suppose that he wouldn't meet with his new contacts, and use their operators, in forty-eight hours at the most."

The Colonel sighed; she was right again. And at a knock on the door he said, "Come."

It was one of the cipher staff, a little slip of a girl wearing very thick horn-rimmed glasses, and her name was Betty something-or-other. She said nervously, "A radio message from Mr. Dekker in France, Colonel. It just came in."

"Who received it?"

"Mr. Foustani, Sir."

"And the hand...did he tell you?"

"He says it was sent by Jill Magran, Sir." She giggled foolishly. "He said her touch stands out like a wart on a flea's nose."

"He's a very poetic man, isn't he?"

But he saw that Vera Vallance was frowning, and he looked at her questioningly. The girl rambled on: "He says it's a very long time since he heard from her in person, but he'd recognize..." She broke off when she saw that Colonel Donovan's thoughts were elsewhere.

"I find that very interesting," Vera said.

"Oh?"

She said carefully, "From what we know of Lievre, he'd never let anyone but his own operators anywhere near his set. If Jill sent it— and I trust Foustani here—it means that Josh has finally decided to reopen contact with us directly, and has recovered his old set."

"*Good*," Wild Bill said emphatically. "In spite of my better judgment, that makes me a very happy man indeed."

He reached for the paper and murmured, "It's, ah, Bessie, is it not?"

She shook her head so vigorously that her glasses almost fell off. "No, Sir. It's Betty."

"Ah yes, of course, how very remiss of me. And you may go now, Betty."

"Yes, Sir, thank you, Sir."

As she scuttled out, Donovan glared at the message and said, "It's very long, for Dekker. Well..."

He read it through very carefully indeed, with no expression at all on his poker face, the one he liked to wear when there was trouble brewing. He handed it at last to Vera, and he said mildly, "Well, we're beginning to learn something, though not enough. And I'm beginning to ask myself just why I ever hired a troublemaker like that damned Dekker. For the past few months, I've merely hated his guts. But now... Maybe I should have Lievre knock him off after all, while there's still a chance. Read it to me, V.V. I've read it thoroughly, and now I want to hear it! I want to hear every nuance in your voice. When he's bullshitting me, when he's being serious. Read it to me."

He put his feet up on the desk, clasped his hands over a paunch that was growing larger by the week with all this desk work, closed his eyes, and listened while Vera read aloud, slowly and deliberately:

DEKKER TO DONOVAN PERSONAL FIRST I THANK YOU FOR YOUR OFFER OF FORGIVENESS TO WHICH MY ANSWER IS GO TO HELL STOP SECOND YOUR BLUEEYED

BOY FERRET IS ON THE POINT OF DEATH AFTER A WEEK WITH THE GESTAPO NO BALLS LEFT AT ALL JUST CHARRED REMAINS AND CAN YOU TELL ME HOW COME HE IS STILL ALIVE STOP THIRD THERE IS STRONG SUSPICION THAT HE WAS DELIBERATELY DROPPED TO THE GERMANS WHICH MEANS IN CASE YOUR LITTLE POINTY HEAD HAS NOT CAUGHT ON BOTH HIS PILOT AND DISPATCH OFFICER SHOULD BE POLITELY QUESTIONED STOP FOURTH SINCE FERRET MAY WELL HAVE DROPPED DEAD WHILE THIS EPIC IS BEING ENCODED SUGGEST YOU INFORM ME OF HIS MISSION AND WITHOUT OBLIGATION ON YOUR PART AND MORE IMPORTANTLY ON MINE I WILL PURSUE IT ONLY BECAUSE THE POOR BASTARD HAS SUFFERED HORRIBLY AND EARNS MY RESPECT JUST BY HIS SURVIVAL AND DETERMINATION STOP FIFTH PLEASE GIVE MY LOVE TO THE BEAUTEOUS VERA AND ENTERTAIN MY SUGGESTION THAT YOU SHOULD SHACK UP WITH HER ONCE IN A WHILE IT MIGHT BE GOOD FOR YOUR SOUL IF YOU HAVE ONE WHICH I DOUBT STOP DO NOT FORGET ABOUT THE PILOT MESSAGE ENDS.

Donovan unfolded himself and sat up. "Well, what do you think?" He was obviously very worried, and Vera said slowly, "Apart from the personal insults, which are in character, I find it very interesting. He's told us a great deal of what we wanted to know, hasn't he?"

"Run a check on that pilot. Better still, have MI6 do it, it might wake them up a bit."

"Okay, I'll see to it. What about the main point of his argument?"

"I am *not*, repeat not, going to pass this mission over to goddam Dekker; the indications are that he's just too chummy with Lievre's Group 47. It'd make hay out of everything we've planned so carefully. Not hay—straw."

"Yes, I think you're right."

"Damn sure I'm right," Donovan growled. "I'll have to send someone else in, and fast. Where's Julius Hammond now?"

"Captain Hammond?" She was startled, and worried too. "He's in Tunisia, but...but surely you're not thinking of sending him, are you?"

"Listen to me, V.V.," the Colonel said sharply. He got to his feet and started prowling around the room. He laid a hand on the block of ice and then cooled his forehead. "I can see all kinds of problems ahead, not excluding the possibility—perhaps even the *probability*—of a stand-up fight between Dekker, aided by Lievre and his group, and whoever takes Ferret's place. And when I say *fight*, I'm not thinking of an exchange of insults. I'm thinking of physical violence, by which I mean guns, knives, whatever. Get Hammond back here right away."

She made one last effort to prevent what she was sure was a mistake—something that Wild Bill Donovan very rarely made.

"The last time," she said, "Hammond lost out to Dekker."

"And ever since," the Colonel said, "he's been waiting to get his own back. This time, believe me, he won't walk in there quite so unprepared. Now for God's sake, pour me a Jack, will you? And you'd better have one yourself."

CHAPTER 6

The time was slipping by fast, and the crucial moment was almost on them. But an unexpected incident gave them all a temporary distraction.

Lievre had sent Roland to the new German camp disguised as a common laborer to work from six in the morning until sunset, for very little money. Roland was, after all, a Frenchman, and the Germans did not like to pay their French labor too much.

And on the first evening, he brought back the news that the delivery of the tree-felling equipment had been held up. It had been sabotaged, it seemed, by another Resistance Group farther to the east, and had been completely destroyed.

"Where?" Lievre asked frowning, and Roland answered, "It was all being sent up from the south, and at a railway siding in Orleans, *somebody* planted *plastiques* in just the right railway wagons. Heavy duty chainsaws, mostly, and it's going to take them a week or more to find replacements."

"Orleans?" Lievre grunted. "That means it was damned Mercier's men."

"Mercier?" Josh Dekker did not know the name, and Lievre said, not at all happily, "You and Donovan know him as Jean Moulin."

"Ah..."

"He's my nemesis, Josh," Lievre said harshly. "He's a good man, there's no doubt about it at all. But he's trying to fake over the whole of the Resistance."

"And didn't you tell me once that you were hoping to do this too?"

63

"Yes, I did, and I'm still hoping. But last year, de Gaulle himself gave Moulin full authority over all the Resistance groups. Over Henri Frenay's *Libération Nationale*, over the Christian Democrats' *Liberté*, over that damned Communist *Libération*; and over my Group 47 too."

He was in a towering rage now, and he went on furiously, "But I'm not going to tip my hat to Jean Moulin or to any other damned bureaucrat who rules from an office instead of in the field!"

"You were right the first time," Dekker said mildly. "From what I've heard, Jean Moulin is a *damned* good man."

"*Bien!* Okay! But I have no intention of becoming third, fourth, fifth, sixth, seventh in command! I will run my own outfit the way I want to run it! With no interference from anyone!"

Dekker had never seen him quite like this; Lievre, usually so sly and quiet, was in a dreadful rage, almost out of control.

And Josh, not known for his sense of fine diplomacy, said quite the wrong thing. "Calm down, Lievre," he murmured: "No one's going to take your gun away from you."

For a moment, Lievre just stared at him, with a very definite hatred for his close friend in his eyes. And then, abruptly, he turned on his heel and stalked away.

Josh Dekker sighed, and went to the cave to find out which of the others were there. He found both the old doctor and Jill Magran crouched over Ferret on his mattress, and he whispered, "How is he?"

The doctor shook his head. "I don't know. He's unconscious again. I gave him massive doses of our digitalis tea, and whether it works or not, who can tell? And whether he'll ever wake up again, that, too, is something I just do not know."

Josh Dekker turned to Jill and held her hand tightly. "And you, my darling?"

She smiled at him. "Fine now, just fine. An hour or so ago, the scar on my breast started turning septic. The doctor here poured hydrogen peroxide all over it, it burns like hell. But it works. Did you talk with Ira?"

"No, not recently."

"He was looking for you."

"Okay, I'll go find him."

But at that moment, Ira Watslaw came into the cave and crouched down beside them, and he said casually, "It's very good that Roland is working on our behalf in that camp. But he's not the only spy we have, did you know that? Monique is there too."

Dekker frowned. "Monique? Who the hell is Monique?"

"Monique Damas," Ira said. "She's the girl Lievre placed in the Marlotte jail. Now that someone has blown the jail to hell and gone with a few well-placed *plastiques*, its Commandant, Captain Otto von Haugwitz, has been transferred there, even though the buildings aren't nearly ready for occupation yet. And he's chosen to take his new companion, our charming Monique, with him."

He lit a cigarette. "Roland brought two of his newfound friends from the camp here this evening, and I've been talking with them. They think I'm a captain in de Gaulle's new army, bless their hearts. And there's only one thing you have to know about Monique. And that is that she works exclusively for money."

"Not the best kind of spy in the world," Josh Dekker said dryly. "But we have to profit by *every* kind, don't we?"

"We do indeed. And with your permission, I thought I'd wander over to the new camp myself in the morning, and see what there is to be seen."

Josh nodded. "A good idea. Maybe Roland can take you there when he reports for work, another laborer."

Ira Watslaw laughed softly. "What both of us could accomplish, as simple working men, Roland and his friends can accomplish by themselves. No. He tells me that von Haugwitz himself is the Senior Officer there, not a single colonel nor even a major posted there yet. It means, Josh, that in my Gestapo Colonel's uniform, I can not only find out about their progress from the Officer in Command himself, I can also scare the shit out of him, something that will give me a great deal of satisfaction."

"Y-e-s." Dekker was very worried. "But don't let your craving for satisfaction cloud your common sense."

"I will never do that, and you know it."

"Yes, I suppose I do. But if we lose you, Ira, we all might as well cut our wrists and the hell with it. Jill, Hugh, Del, Mike, and me too, we all depend on you more heavily than you'll ever believe."

"As you do in this case," the Pole said mildly. "And all it really needs is someone whose German is better than the German they speak themselves. Tomorrow morning, Josh, we can learn a great deal from my upcoming conversation with Hauptmann Otto von Haugwitz."

"Okay," Josh Dekker said tightly. "Just don't push it too hard."

"That," Ira said, "is also something I never do. I make it a matter of principle to know the limits of my enemies' competence. And more importantly, perhaps, to know my own. Good night, Josh."

He was gone.

And during the long night, disaster struck at young Monique Damas.

It was nearly three o'clock in the morning when Monique lay wide awake in her bed in the servants' dormitory, preparing her report for Roland by the meager light of a small candle.

She was safe here—she thought.

All the female servants in this vast and barren temporary hut were French, eighteen of them all told, sleeping on cold army cots and eating German rations, which were very heavy on boiled cabbage, boiled potatoes, and boiled sausages.

But the Germans were not always foolish, and they had infiltrated two of their own French spies here, women who were anxious to join the Fascist *Milice* when it finally got going, either for money or to further their pro-German thinking.

One of them was named Mathilde Valois, a farmer's wife who was convinced—as her husband was—that France was being taken over by the Communists and that only the Germans could save the country from this dreadful fate.

Mathilde was watching the faint glow of the candle, four beds down from her own. She gave Monique time to hang herself if, indeed, this was what she was doing.

And then, she made up her mind, tossed back the coarse linen sheet, and strode over to Monique's bed.

She snatched the paper from Monique's hand, and struck the poor girl across the face, very hard, when she tried to recover it. She read it through, very carefully, and she said at last, "Yes. It's what I thought it would be. And now, you will come with me, my girl."

She was a peasant woman, and very strong. She dragged Monique from her cot, twisted her arm up behind her back, grabbed a handful of her hair, and marched her off.

Outside, she said to the Corporal on guard there, "I am Mathilde, working with *Hauptmann* von Haugwitz. Take me to him."

When he hesitated, she screamed, "I have captured a spy! Take me to the Captain!"

He slung his machine pistol over his shoulder, and escorted them to the Captain's temporary quarters.

It was half-past six in the morning when a Gestapo colonel, a casual cigarette at his lips, strolled through the gate to the vast new complex that was just in the early stages of construction. He acknowledged the Heil Hitlers of the guards there with a careless wave of the hand, and he found a *Feldwebel* supervising some digging by a dozen or so French laborers. Roland was one of them, though the phony Colonel paid him no attention at all.

It was Ira Watslaw in his favorite disguise, and as he approached, the *Feldwebel* snapped to rigid attention and shot out his right arm, "Heil Hitler!"

"Yes, of course," Ira said languidly, "let's all heil the ass of *der Fuhrer*, I'm sure he'll relish it. But meanwhile, I am looking for your Commanding Officer, Captain von Haugwitz?"

"He is in his hut, Herr *Oberst*, over there."

"Well, get him for me, idiot!"

"*Jawohl*, Herr *Oberst*, *sofort*, at once!"

He scurried off, and in a moment or two the Captain came hurrying, wondering why it could be that so exalted a personage as a Gestapo colonel should be calling on him at such an ungodly hour of the morning; he was also worried because he had not yet shaved.

He stood at rigid attention and gave the mandatory salute, which Ira Watslaw ignored altogether. Instead, he murmured, "We of the Gestapo High Command are to have quarters here too, are you aware of that, Captain?"

"Yes, Sir."

"I myself will command the small detachment of officers stationed here."

"Yes, Sir."

Haugwitz was worried; he had previously been told that the Gestapo would be headed by a mere captain, and this change in the High Command's plans made him nervous. Not only was he hoping for this post himself, but he also felt very uncomfortable with senior officers breathing down his neck, it was just too damned inhibiting.

The Colonel was saying, "I've been waiting for a very long time to escape the noise, the bustle, the smells of the city, and this delay causes me very little pleasure, I assure you."

"But...but Herr *Oberst*. With respect, Sir," the Captain stammered, "it's a matter quite beyond my own control, our heavy equipment was sabotaged—"

"I know that, you foolish fellow. But surely it can be replaced very easily?"

"It has all been requisitioned Sir, but it seems that the engineers are not very anxious to resupply us. I have been told, however, that the new equipment has been released, and will be delivered to us very shortly now."

"And what do you call 'very shortly'? A day or two, a week, a month?" Ira Watslaw asked, and the Captain said at once, "The new schedule, Herr *Oberst*, calls for the clearing of the land at the western extremity of the gorge to begin by next Wednesday. The oaks there are very large, and it will take us three days to cut and stump them. The prefabricated buildings are already on the site, as the Herr *Oberst* will have seen, and it will take us an estimated six days to erect them all. This means, Sir, that in a little less than three weeks from today, the new camp will be ready for occupation. The water lines are already in over sixty percent of the area, twelve of the fourteen cesspools have already been dug, and most of the electricity is ready."

The Colonel interrupted him. "Show me," he said, "that part of the camp which has already been partly completed."

And for the next two hours, the Captain gave him the benefit of a guided tour, and Ira Watslaw made a mental note of every watchtower, every checkpoint, every machine-gun and anti-aircraft revetment, every main and subsidiary command post, of every storage facility for weapons and ammunition, of every temporary mess hall and barracks, of every parking area for the personnel carriers, light tanks, trucks, and other transport, of each and every foxhole and floodlight by the fencing around the perimeter.

Inevitably, the question of defense against sneak attacks came up, and Ira said nonchalantly, "It seems that you are well protected against any effort by the Resistance to disrupt your work here."

The Captain felt he was on very safe ground now, and he said, beaming, "Not only in our ground defenses, Herr *Oberst*, but in our counterintelligence as well. We have more than a hundred and twenty French men and women working here, most of them, I am sure, on our side. But to guard against those who are not, I have three female and two male spies of my own working among them."

"Excellent," the Colonel murmured, and Haugwitz went on: "I am happy to report, Sir, that one of them, by name Mathilde Valois, caught a Resistance spy during the night, caught her in the act of writing a report to a man named Lievre, who heads Group 47."

"I know who Lievre is."

"Yes, Sir. She brought this girl to me, together with the beginnings of her report which indicates that there is another of their spies in the camp."

"Not entirely surprising."

"No Sir. His code-name seems to be Roland, we're looking through the lists of our male employees now in the hopes of identifying him."

"And the girl?"

"One of our mess waitresses, Herr *Oberst*. Her name is Monique Damas, she came to us from the jail in Marlotte, which I personally find very interesting, since it was from Marlotte that the American spy Ferret was abducted. It's possible that this adds up to a very interesting conclusion."

There was a dreadful tingling sensation at the back of Ira Watslaw's scalp, but he controlled himself with an effort and said, very quietly, "And you have sent her, I imagine, back to our headquarters in Paris for interrogation?"

"Not yet, Herr *Oberst*," the Captain said. "I'm sending her back under heavy guard with the daily courier, who..." He looked at his watch. "Who leaves in an hour and a half from now."

"And meanwhile?"

"She's in my temporary quarters, Colonel, in my hut."

There was a little moment of silence, and then Captain Otto von Haugwitz said, seizing the opportunity, "When I was posted here, Herr *Oberst*, his Excellency, General von Einstadt himself indicated to me that the completion of the new camp might bring me promotion and a position of greater authority here, which is much to be desired. Therefore, I have always been anxious to impress upon my superiors my...my great *dedication* to my work."

"I want to see this girl," Ira Watslaw said, and the Captain nodded. "This way, Sir."

"I will not be necessary to send her to town. I will take her there myself."

"Of course. I will provide the Herr *Oberst* with an escort."

"That will not be necessary. I have my own bodyguards on the road."

"Yes, I understand."

As they walked together past the rows of barracks to the officers' quarters, the Captain said, rambling on and hoping to curry yet more favor from this high-ranking officer, "It seemed wise to me not to waste the early hours of the morning, Herr *Oberst*. First, because this is the time during which suspects are at their most vulnerable. And secondly, there is the other psychological advantage, which is the great fear at the moment of arrest. We must take advantage of it before it dissipates, before a sort of protective instinct builds up to form a barrier that might well be impenetrable."

"You are truly a thinking man, Haugwitz," Ira said caustically, "aren't you?" and the Captain beamed.

"I have a doctorate in psychology from Heidelberg, Herr *Oberst*," he said smugly, thinking only of promotion. "And so, I took it upon myself to begin her interrogation personally."

"Oh?" There was that curdling of the blood again.

"And just what have you done to her, Haugwitz?"

The Captain shrugged. "So far, she's lost only her fingernails. She had very little else to lose; she's a whore."

The Pole fought against the trembling that seized him; it was too close to home. And he said tightly, "And what has she told you?"

"As yet, nothing at all. She just screams a great deal. But without a doubt, in Paris, they'll find the means to break her."

They had come to the Captain's hut, and as they entered, the Captain said, "When I'd left her, she'd fainted. But I'm sure she's recovered by now."

The hut was a very simple place to call a home and an office. Built of plywood panels, it was some sixteen feet square, with a small shower and toilet and a galley kitchen attached to it.

It was furnished with a big plank-and-trestle table, an open cupboard containing an incongruous mass of papers, dishes, bottles, and glasses, with half a dozen camp chairs and a camp cot in one corner, its blankets folded with the most meticulous military precision and with a footlocker where it belonged.

There was a *Feldwebel* there, a Sergeant, springing instantly to attention and shouting "Heil Hitler" as they entered.

And at the plank table, Monique Damas was seated, quite naked.

"I stripped her," Captain von Haugwitz said. "They're always more vulnerable when they don't have the protection of clothing." (He was one hell of a psychologist.)

But her head was resting on the table between her outstretched arms, as though she were unconscious.

Her hands, knuckles up, were nailed to the table, two four-inch spikes driven into each of them. And her fingertips were a bloodied mess. The pliers lay there, mute evidence.

This was a very common Gestapo method of what they called 'persuasion.' (They never liked to use the word torture.) And for more than three hours, Monique had suffered it as the stolid Sergeant, just doing what he was ordered to do, slowly—very slowly—tore out her fingernails one by one.

For three hours and more, the interrogation had gone on:

"Where is your Commanding Officer Lievre at this moment?

"Who is your contact in this camp?

"What is the military strength of your Group 47?

"Is this maniac Dekker working for Group 47, or are they working for him?

"Is Lievre joining forces with the southern groups of the Resistance, or not?"

And through all of this, Captain von Haugwitz had heard nothing from her except her prolonged and anguished screaming.

Now, Ira Watslaw lifted her head up gently, and as gently lowered it back into place again; he could not hide his trembling.

The Captain stared, and he stammered, "But...But Herr *Oberst*, when I left her, she was...she was still alive! Unconscious, yes, but...but still breathing."

For a very long time, the Pole was silent, and he was thinking not only of Monique, but also of the terrible days in Warsaw, far behind him now in everything but cruel memory. He went to the window and stared out at the troops drilling there, going through unarmed combat under the careful scrutiny of a brawny sergeant whose brutal face was scarred with long-forgotten knife wounds.

He thought of others he had known who had survived far worse than this, and of still others who had died from the shock and the awful pain of far less.

He turned and went back to the table, searing the sight of her into his mind forever, something else to add to the long list of personal tragedies he would never allow himself to forget, *ever*.

Vaguely, he heard the Captain blustering. "It is regrettable; Herr *Oberst*, of course. And I must...I must accept responsibility. But the Colonel will agree, I am sure, that this could not..." He swallowed hard, and saw his hoped for promotion vanishing. "...this could not have been foreseen, under any circumstances. And she was...she was only a whore, as I personally know."

Ira had taken a fountain pen from the breast pocket of his uniform and was twiddling it almost absently between his fingers. He saw that both the Captain and the Sergeant were terrified, the Sergeant still standing at rigid attention, the Officer gesturing helplessly as he sought for words and could not find them.

He held the pen in his right hand, lightly, as though using it as a pointer to emphasize what he was about to say, though he, too, was unable to find the words. He depressed the clip twice in rapid succession, sending a stream of cyanide gas into two faces that had no time even to show their consternation. There was a dreadful choking sound, and he fired twice more for good measure, even though he knew that it was unnecessary.

As they hit the ground and twisted their bodies in the last, frantic convulsions, he placed a hand on Monique's tousled head and held it there for a moment. And then, he went outside into the filtered sunlight of the beautiful forested gorge, and closed the door quietly behind him.

As he walked through the trees and the buildings, among the troops and the laborers, he saw that a squat and thickset peasant woman was watching him. She had seen him leave the Captains hut, without a doubt, and he wondered about it.

But she was grinning at him, a little stupidly, and when he held her look she wiped her hands on her skirt and approached him.

Had she been waiting there for him? He stopped.

She said in French, grimacing: "I do not speak German, M'sieur *le Colonel*, only French."

He answered her in her own language. "And so? What is it you want, woman?"

"Ah." She was glad of his fluency, and she said, with peasant bluntness. "What every French man or woman wants in these hard times. A little money, not very much."

Could she have seen what had happened? Through the window, where he had been standing only moments before the killing? He quickly dismissed the possibility, and he said coldly, "And why should I give you money?"

"Because it was I who caught your spy for you," she said eagerly. "I am one of the spies *Leutnant* Mansfeld placed in the camp, working for those who have come to save France from the Communists."

"Ah, I see."

"I would ask Captain von Haugwitz himself, but..." There was a wide shrug. "The Captain never wants to speak with women who look like me, only if they are young and pretty; you must know how he is."

"Yes. I know exactly how he is."

"Well then?"

"Tell me your name."

"My name is Mathilde, Mathilde Valois. I caught the spy in the middle of the night, writing a report for the Resistance, and took her myself to the Captain."

"Then you must indeed be rewarded," Ira Watslaw said. "Come with me, my good woman..."

He took her to a remote corner of the gorge where his stolen German staff car was parked. There were two dead bodies, a Gestapo Captain and his soldier servant, carefully hidden under the gorse bushes by Route N 51 where it flanked The Rocks of the Young Ladies, to attest to the hijacking. A worried Mike Homer was at the wheel, wearing the uniform of a German corporal, even though his knowledge of the language, improving fast in a self-taught kind of fashion, was not very good.

There was the little flag on its front left fender which identified the vehicle as belonging to a senior officer of the Gestapo—enough to ensure that every lesser German mortal would give it as wide a berth as possible. Nonetheless, Mike was nursing his silent little Anderson gun, as well as his Schmeisser machine pistol and four of the German stick grenades for use in any real emergency.

He saw the look on Ira Watslaw's face, and wisely said nothing as he leaped out of the car and opened the rear door for the Colonel and this uncouth-looking peasant woman. He listened to the French conversation going on in the back there as they turned west on the Route Ronde, and he understood at least some of it.

And there was no one happier than Mike Homer when they finally arrived at the cave which had become, for the moment, the headquarters of Lievre's Group 47, and therefore of Dekker's freebooters too.

At last, Mike was able to relax, and he said with a sigh of relief, "Thank God! I've never been so shit scared in my life! A patrol passed by while you were gone, Ira, and they *questioned* me, can you believe it? I just sat there and stared straight ahead, wouldn't answer a single question, largely because I didn't know what the fuck they were talking about. And at last, I just pointed to the flag we were flying, and they got the point and pissed off, highly unsatisfied with a very unproductive encounter."

Josh Dekker and Lievre were there, and it seemed that they

were friends again.

Staring at Mathilde, Lievre said: "*Et la femme*? Who's the woman you bring so carelessly into the camp, Ira? I hope you know what you're doing, the risks you run?"

"No risks at all," Ira Watslaw said tightly. "Her name is Mathilde Valois. And she's been a spy, working for the Gestapo in the camp. What is more, she turned Monique Damas over to Captain von Haugwitz, who is now dead. But so, I'm afraid, is Monique. She died under torture." His voice rose, and he said harshly, "I give her to you. Lievre, she's yours now. Just let us know what she has to say, is it a deal?"

"It's a deal," Lievre said. "You have my word."

He took her arm and helped her out of the car, and he said gently, "Come, Mathilde, come with me. It seems that we have a great deal to talk about."

Silently, he led her away.

They sat together in the beautiful forest, eating sandwiches and drinking wine, and it might have been a friendly picnic, save for the three guards standing at a distance with their rifles ready. And. Mathilde was slowly losing the great fear that had been clutching at her heart.

But it returned in full force when Lievre said, very gently, "Do you know what the Resistance does with traitors, Mathilde?"

She swallowed hard. "I know that you torture them."

"I have dealt harshly with other men, on occasion," Lievre said. "Never a woman. It is only your life that is at stake now. Tell me why it is that you are working for the *Bosches*. Is it for money?"

Recovering a little, she mumbled; "What money? The money means very little. It is little, and therefore it *means* little."

"For what, then? A philosophy? Are you a Fascist?"

"I Hate the Communists. I am not a Fascist."

"What has communism got to do with this?"

She was plucking up her courage again. "You're the Resistance, *n'est-ce-pas*?"

Lievre said patiently, "The Communists in the Resistance are almost all with de la Vigerie's *Libération*, and I will have nothing whatsoever to do with them. Indeed, I hate them almost as much as I hate the Germans."

"They told me you were all Communists."

"They?"

"The Germans."

"They lied."

"As you lie now."

He said very quietly, "I tell you once again, Mathilde, your life is at stake."

She was a simple woman, but not without courage. "I will tell you nothing," she said bluntly.

There was a little silence, and then, "Did you know that Monique the woman you betrayed, was killed? That she died under torture?"

"I don't care. She was a whore and a Communist."

Lievre controlled himself. "How many others of your kind are there in the camp? Working for the Germans?"

"I just said, I will tell you nothing."

"Their names can save your life now."

Her voice was rising, "Go on, torture me, too. Stick needles in my breasts the way men of the Gestapo do, you're no better than they are!" She said furiously, "I don't care what you do to me, can you understand that?"

There was a dreadful weight on Lievre's unhappy shoulders. He knew well that women like this were not uncommon, women who would never be broken. He looked into her eyes and saw nothing but defiance there, and he said harshly, "You leave me with no alternative, Mathilde. I must sentence you to death."

There was no expression on her face at all as he stood up and began to move away. He turned back, and he said very quietly, "Your last chance, Mathilde. Will you change your mind?"

Contemptuously, she tossed the rest of her sandwich away for the birds to find and to feed on, and emptied the remainder of the wine in her mug onto the grasses of the forest floor.

She stood up and held her head high, and she said, "I will wait for you in hell, pig. It won't be a long wait, I'm sure of it."

Lievre caught the eye of one of the guards, and nodded.

As he moved away, he heard the single shot which, he knew, would have gone straight through the center of Mathilde Valois's forehead.

He did not look back.

CHAPTER 7

It was very early in the morning when Gilbert Favre, code-named Chien after his passion for dogs, came to where Lievre was just tucking his blanket away into its habitual hiding place, and whispered, "We have to talk. Not here."

He was just a boy, no more than eighteen years old, and he was the head of Lievre's radio group, not only the best of the operators, but also trusted with the coding and decoding of the messages that were constantly going back and forth, to and from Cairo and London, and sometimes to other Resistance groups as well.

He was bright and articulate, well-educated, the son of a banker who had been shot as a hostage by the Gestapo, and had himself been wounded twice in skirmishes with German troops. As usual, there was a small puppy at his heels, one of the many strays abandoned in the forest ever since their owners, hungry themselves, had not been able to care for their pets. It was not a cruel fate; the dogs soon became expert at feeding themselves on rabbits, weasels, foxes, and careless birds, and there was water everywhere.

He turned and moved away with an extraordinary animal kind of lope, and Lievre followed him till they came to a small bluff overlooking the Bouligny Rocks. They sat there together, just below the skyline and well-concealed from any German binoculars by a dense stand of hazel saplings. They listened for a moment to the friendly sounds of the birds breaking the silence and the rustle of the wind in the leaves.

Gilbert said quietly. "Foustani came on the air at three o'clock this morning with a message for me."

"For you personally?"

He nodded. "We've been signaling each other for so long now that he's come to regard me as a close personal friend, which I am not, I don't like traitors. And between you and me, I sometimes suspect that he's not only working for Donovan and secretly for us, but that he's also in the pay of the Germans."

He lit a Gauloise cigarette and puffed on it, sending little spirals of blue smoke twisting away on the breeze as Lievre waited. Then he went on. "That man is fantastic with the key, but when it comes to encoding a message, even with the simple code he has, half of the time he fucks it up. But I spent the early hours of the morning in clarification, asking a lot of questions. My God, I had to change frequency four times, I won't stay that long on the air with just one. Finally, I got it all worked out. And it's pretty lousy news, *mon Commandant.*"

"Go on," Lievre said.

"First of all, Captain Hammond is coming back here. You remember Hammond? From the Catinat days?"

Lievre frowned. "Of course. But, he's not going to try and take over from Dekker again, is he? The way I remember it, he damn nearly got killed the last time."

"Not from Dekker. From Ferret."

"I see. Well, that should prove interesting."

"And there's more to come. We know what's in that famous suitcase. Two million dollars in Swiss currency."

Lievre said calmly, "And since Ferret has been so secretive about it, we can assume that it's not for us, right?"

"It's not," Gilbert said. "It's for Jean Moulin."

"*What?*"

"For Jean Moulin's *Combat.* It seems Donovan thinks they're the up-and-coming group, and he's switching his allegiance."

The hell with distant binoculars, Lievre was on his feet and striding back and forth like a caged panther, and he said furiously, not even keeping his voice low, "Over my dead body!"

He was quite paranoid about his rival, and he was in an overpowering rage now. It was not true to say that he had foreseen this, but he had feared the loss of his power for a very long time now, ever since de Gaulle had given Jean Moulin the overall mandate that had made him—if only in theory—the head of all the Resistance.

And he hated it, with a passionate loathing.

"Sit down," Gilbert said. "You're on the skyline."

Lievre sat, and when the puppy came and licked his hand, he pushed it away angrily and growled, "Get away from me, you damn dog. I don't need your sympathy."

With a sigh, Gilbert picked the puppy up, placed it on his knees, and stroked it gently. "And yet," he said, "it's not as bad as it might be, is it? After all, between us, Dekker's people and ours, we're going to retrieve that suitcase, are we not? And you and I both know whose hands it's going to finish up in, don't we?"

Lievre was fast recovering his calm as he thought about it. He nodded. "Yes, of course. But still, a nasty problem remains."

"Which is?"

"Does Josh Dekker know all this? Or does he not? He's using his old radio now; Donovan may have told him."

Gilbert shook his head. "No, I think not. He's clever, and he's tough. But he's still a naive American, and if he knew, he would surely have given some sign of it by now. He's not a devious man at all, just not emotionally capable of hiding a thing like this."

"I count him as a friend, a friend I trust my life to, and yet," he grimaced. "And yet, reason tells me that the moment I start trusting anybody in France today, I am writing my own death certificate. And if I find out he's been fooling me..."

He fell silent, knowing that the discovery of the truth would not be easy. He thought about it for a long time, and then he murmured, "Jill Magran is his weakest link, did you know that?"

Gilbert stared at him for a moment, and then his face creased up in a wide and boyish grin, and he said, laughing, "Jill? She's tougher than any of them! And she's his girlfriend too, for God's sake!"

"Once," Lievre said, "she was very nearly mine. I just didn't...didn't push hard enough. There's got to be a way! And after all, she's more French than she is American! If, this time, I can find the right words..."

He knew of Dekker's very strong love for her, of its origins, its loss, and its rediscovery some ten years or more later. Jill herself had told him, in one of their rare confidences together, how Josh had taken her virginity when she was only fifteen years old, and in the back seat of a Chevy! She had told him how he had found her again, quite by chance when, after that long separation, he had come across her in Cairo, where she was teaching unarmed combat to the paratroopers and commandos of de Gaulle's new army. (She was damned good at it too. She had demonstrated for his benefit by disarming him of both pistol and dagger and hurling him over her shoulder as though he was a weakling—three times in a row and with no effort at all.)

He thought of their first frustrated moments of intimacy, when she had masturbated him by the bank of the River Seine in Paris. Of the time he had tried to persuade her, as a Frenchwoman, to leave Dekker and to join his own Group 47.

And he knew that deep in her heart, she still held a strange, divided affection for him.

He said again, roughly: "She's a woman. There's got to be a way."

The day was cloudy, and summer rain was threatening, casting the Gorge aux Loups into dark and somber shadows.

On the high rocks just across Route 58, that led from Marlotte to Fontainebleau itself, Josh Dekker and Ira Watslaw sat together with Lievre high above the road and the German camp beyond it, watching the laborers at work on the construction. They were less than a mile away, and through their powerful Leitz binoculars they were studying the activity down there as Ira pointed out the various buildings that had already been completed in the eastern sector—the stores, the officers' quarters, the men's barracks, the tall watch-towers. They studied the positions of the defensive barricades, the revetted gun posts with their artillery pieces in place, and the machine-gun nests, well-placed and in great quantity.

There were the 7.5cm Field Guns as well as the formidable 15cm howitzers, the light 5cm mortars which the German Army had consistently used with such deadly effect, as well as 3.7cm antitank guns and huge piles of the *handgranate* stick mortars all stacked in

Germanic precision.

At the southeastern comer, where the approach to the complex seemed to be the most feasible, a row of some forty heavy mortars had been set up, and Josh said quietly, "Scrub any attack on the southeast, Lievre. Take a look at the mortars there, that's the eight centimeter thirty-four, I think. And it's deadly."

Lievre trained his glasses on them. "Yes," he whispered, "that's what they are."

"Range of more than twenty-six hundred yards," Ira murmured.

"I know," Lievre said. "But get within sixty meters of them—and they're too close to be of any use. And don't try and give me instructions in tactics, Josh. We'll be a lot closer than sixty meters when we start firing."

"For a man who doesn't need any suggestions," Josh said tartly, "you're not very bright, are you? What happens when you start to retreat, you want to tell me that?"

Lievre bit his lip. "Okay, okay," he said. "But I'm far more worried about what's happening at the western end. I've a nasty feeling you're walking into a lot of trouble there."

"And *I've* a nasty feeling that you're right."

"Something I didn't count on," Ira Watslaw said tightly. "I should have thought of it, I'm sorry."

The heavy equipment the late Captain von Haugwitz had been waiting for had still not arrived. But the oaks at the eastern extremity of the gorge were being marked now, surveying equipment was being setup everywhere, foxholes were being dug, and three personnel carriers were stationed there. Moreover, some thirty or forty troopers were standing around, seemingly idle, and all armed with the MG34 light machine-gun—a far more potent weapon than their normal Schmeisser, and a matter that gave Josh Dekker a problem.

He said, muttering, "Are they *expecting* an attack at this end of the gorge? That looks to me like one hell of a lot of firepower to defend a few goddamn surveyors. Do we have a leak somewhere?"

Lievre was trying to convince himself as much as anyone else. "Not among my people," he said. "I completely trust everyone who knows of this operation."

He remembered his comment to the young Gilbert. *The moment I start trusting anybody in France today, I am writing my own death certificate.* But now, since Foustani's message, he wanted that suitcase more than anything in the world.

He was a man accustomed to making quick decisions in an emergency, and he said to Dekker: "We'll have to move the operation forward, Josh. You can't afford to wait for them to get stronger, as they undoubtedly will."

"Agreed, one hundred percent. Can you be ready by tonight?"

"Yes."

"The moon sets," Ira Watslaw said, "at three-thirteen. That'll give us two and a half hours before first light."

"Okay. Let's get back to the safe-house."

Josh Dekker and Hugh Black were in quiet conference together, sorting out the specialized equipment they would need for the operation—the long nylon ropes with their tiny anchors attached, the Anderson guns that were silenced to an incredible degree by the addition of a wire baffle to the barrel, the hand crossbows no bigger than a small pistol and powered by ordinary rubber slingshot tubing that could hurl an eight-inch dart for more than two hundred yards, the spike knuckle dusters.

They were to carry their Schmeisser machine pistols as well, since they were all to be dressed in German uniform and this would be expected of them. And, had all their secret auxiliary weapons not been concealed under their clothing, they would have looked like walking arsenals.

Ira Watslaw, who was once again to be the Gestapo Colonel, was busy in his own comer of the cave, sketching from memory an excellent depiction of all the various German strongpoints that would interest Lievre's men when they opened their diversionary attack. Mike Homer and Del Adam were wrestling together, practicing the French system of self-defense called *savate*—largely a matter of attack with the feet—which Jill Magran had taught them.

And Jill was taking a bath in a small pool Lievre had showed her only a few hundred yards below the cave. The water was ice cold and very refreshing, and she was splashing it over her healing wounds.

And then, she suddenly became aware that she was not alone.

There was no sound, not even the rustle of a dried leaf or the movement of a bush, but she was certain, certain with an instinctive feeling of the kind that always comes to those who spend their days and nights in constant danger.

She made no hasty movement at all, not even to cover herself, Instead, she stood up and splashed her way quite slowly to where she had left the French peasant clothes she had taken to wearing at the safe-house, very conscious of her own body but knowing that any sign of caution now would betray her. She also knew that her Anderson gun and her dagger were both concealed under the heavy woolen skirt that lay on the rocks there, the gun ready for instant firing, its safety catch off.

And then, she saw him.

It was Lievre himself, rising up from concealment under the shrubbery not more than a half-dozen paces away, and he stood there staring at her, a very slight smile on his face as he studied her intently, his eyes devouring her, the firm breasts, the long smooth thighs, the small triangle of silky hair, almost the color of autumn leaves, and then, at last, her eyes.

She bent down slowly to retrieve her panties and stepped into them, then put on her skirt and slipped the cotton-blouse over her head; then she just stood there looking at him silently, and he came to her and took both her hands in his.

He said, very quietly, "You know, you *must* know, how deeply I've always felt for you. And yet, in all this time, I've only once before seen you naked."

"Oh? Once before? And when was that?" She was very calm.

"At the safe-house in Paris. It was a hot and very sultry night, and the cellar was intolerably stuffy. Everyone was asleep, it was the early hours of the morning, and I'd come to talk with Josh. But I didn't like to wake him, and you. You had thrown open your sleeping bag, and you were directly under the single shaded bulb you always kept alight, you remember? I thought then, as I think now, that I had never seen any woman so beautiful."

"And how long have you been watching me?"

"From the moment you arrived here. I wanted to feast my eyes on you."

"That wasn't very proper of you, Alphonse."

They were speaking French, and he was glad that she called him by his own name, which the others surely must have forgotten, if they'd ever known it. He said, "It's hard to be in love and be...*proper.*"

"Yes, I suppose that's true. And you came down here just to look at me?"

"To look at you. To touch you. But most of all...to talk with you."

His hand moved to rest very lightly on her breast. She made no motion to restrain him, and he felt the tiny nipple hardening under his touch. His other arm was about her, holding her body tight against his, and he fancied he could feel her trembling too.

"No," she whispered. "No, Alphonse, you must not. Tell me instead what it is you want to talk to me about."

His hand slipped under the cotton of her blouse to caress her, the touch of a butterfly's wing; still she did not move to stop him. Instead, she whispered, with a touch of desperation in her voice, "Please, Alphonse, please? You know about Josh and me."

"Yes. I know that you're his girl. But once, you were almost mine, you remember?"

His hand at her breast was stronger now, and he was holding her tighter still, pushing her loins into his so that she could feel the strength in his penis. She was breathing quite heavily now, and beginning to struggle against him, but only a little, and he said, pressing hard, "You remember that night in Paris? By the riverbank?"

"Yes, I remember it. It must not happen again."

"Are you ashamed of it?"

"I was then, perhaps, just a little. Not any longer. Even though... It's strange, isn't it? Back then, I wasn't truly Josh's woman, and now, I am. And Josh. He's your friend! You can't do this to him, you mustn't!"

"And yet, I have a feeling that if I tried to force you, I might succeed, without too much damage done to either of us. Am I right, dear Jill?"

She was a frank and honest woman, never capable of deceiving herself, and she shook her head, tossing back her hair. "I don't know," she said, "I just don't know. If I chose to fight you, you know I'm capable of it, I'm as strong as you are. But for you, for me, for Josh, yes, for all the others, it would never be the same for us again."

Now, at last, she pulled his probing hand away, and she said quietly, "Even if I decided, out of shame, to try and hide it from Josh, which I probably would not do, he'd find out, one way or another. And then...then he'd kill you."

Lievre said, smiling now, "Or I would have to kill him."

"Either of which outcome is not a possibility I want to face."

"Very well." He clasped his hands at her back, lightly now so that the awful pressure was almost gone, and he said, "Then tell me one thing, and I will say no more."

"Which is?"

"Deep down in your heart, don't you feel anything for me?"

"A very strong affection, Alphonse. It's just not strong enough to betray Josh."

"Then I am satisfied. I will not try to force myself on you, you have my word."

He kissed her quickly on both cheeks, and as he took her arm and turned away with her, Jill could not decide for the life of her whether the strange, insistent feeling that came over her was one of relief, or of utter frustration.

"Come," he said, very much in control now, "I'll walk you back to the cave."

And as they walked slowly over the broken ground, dotted here and there with gorse, and hazel, and a dozen other kinds of trees and bushes, he came to the subject he was really interested in. And still, he approached it very slowly, even though they had reached the degree of intimacy he thought would make speaking easier.

He said somberly, "It's going to be a rough battle tonight, and Josh tells me his whole group is going, including you. I don't quite see why. There's no work for a woman here, the way there was in the Catinat case."

"I'm not going as a woman," Jill said. "I'm going as a fighter, equal to the rest of them, maybe even better than any of them, including Josh. And I've been delegated to look after Ferret in case he doesn't make it. I can't believe the extent of his recovery; the man's a walking corpse. But I'm staying beside him at all times in case he collapses."

"And if he does?"

"Then Mike takes over; and carries him home. Or at least, out of the immediate danger." She shrugged. "I could probably do that, too, if I put my mind to it, but Josh says no."

"And if he dies?"

"Then we have to leave him there. It's sad, but that's the way it has to be. They can't hurt him any more once he's dead."

"I hate it."

"The chances are there won't be any fighting at all, not for us. You're the one who's taking all the risks. We ought to be home free."

Now was the moment... As casually as he could manage, Lievre said: "I can't help wondering what's in that suitcase," and Jill said at once, "*Money*."

He pulled up short. "Then you do know!"

She turned to stare at him. "Know? Know what?"

"About Jean Moulin and his *Combat*."

Her mouth was open wide, and he was watching her closely. She said, utterly bewildered, "But... but what the hell has Jean Moulin got to do with this?"

Now answering her, he said softly, "How did you know about the money?"

"For God's sake, Alphonse! What the hell's going on here? If it's something we should know about—"

"How did you know?"

"Jesus!" She threw up her arms. "Of course there's got to be money there, a lot of money! You remember when we landed? Josh was carrying almost nothing but the money, I was carrying the radio, and everything else was in Hugh Black's containers. Ferret was alone, so he'd have been carrying just the radio and the cash, the two things he can't do without! It's obvious."

He held her look for a long time. And he *knew* knew for certain, that she was not putting on an act. He took a long deep breath and said, a last effort, "Then Josh doesn't know either?"

Jill said irritably, "Josh knows what I know, I know what he knows, no more, no less. We have no secrets, we never had secrets between us. And now, for Christ's sake, tell me about Jean Moulin!"

Lievre put his arms around her, and he said, very earnestly, "First, *mon amour*, I must ask your forgiveness for my suspicions. But for a while I was beginning to believe—I had *reason* to believe—that my best friend, Josh Dekker, was trying to deceive me, in the name of...of loyalty to Colonel Donovan."

"To *Donovan*? Are you crazy?"

"Yes, I was a fool, I admit it. If too much caution can be considered foolish. But..." He sighed.

"Donovan in Cairo has his spies in France. We in France have our spies in Cairo..."

He went on to tell her the whole story of Foustani's messages, and she listened intently. And when he had finished, he said, worried about it, "When Josh gets that suitcase tonight... I'm going to have to take it from him."

Jill shook her head, and he felt the muscles around his jaw tightening. But she went on, speaking with absolute certainty: "You *won't*, Alphonse. Josh will simply...just give it to you, freely. After he's checked it out, of course."

"Are you sure of that?"

"He's as devoted to Group 47 as you are. And as devoted to you personally, as I am."

He held her tightly and kissed her. And in a little while, they found Josh Dekker at the hideout, took him aside and well out of anyone else's hearing, like Ferret's, told him the news.

CHAPTER 8

Shortly after noon, Roland had taken his bicycle and had gone from the new safe-house to the old—to the cellar of the restaurant on rue de la Sourdiere in Paris named The Laughing Pig.

It was owned by Madame Yvonne Fermont, a senior officer in Lievre's Group 47 and also mistress to General Hans von Einstadt, the elderly head of the Gestapo's northern sector.

He was carrying messages for her from Lievre. It was a trip he made twice weekly, taking a different route each time.

That evening, with sentries posted everywhere around the hideout, Dekker and his squad of freebooters were sitting under the trees and eating a dinner of rabbit stew that had been slowly braised in a sauce made from tomatoes, onions, fennel, and wine, and then sprinkled over with wild thyme. The sun was just going down.

As the shadows lengthened, one of the guards came hurrying to them, grinning broadly and saying, "Look who tried to sneak past my post."

Josh leaped to his feet and held out his arms, a tremendous delight showing on his face. "Yvonne!" he said, "just a few weeks and it feels like months, no, years! And how are you, my love?"

"Fine, just fine." She was a little out of breath as they all embraced her, beaming at her and whispering all kinds of foolish endearments, and Lievre said happily: "I wish you'd sent word you were coming, I'd have broken out the best china."

"To say nothing of the crystal and the silver," Hugh Black added. "Sit down and eat with us. Not quite the kind of food we've been used to at the Cochon, but adequate, I think."

Del Adam was already slicing up meat with his favorite knife and piling it up onto a tin plate for her, and she said, savoring the ripeness coming from the pot: "A little nutmeg would have worked wonders with it. Yes, I'll eat with you, I'm famished."

Mike Homer passed her a mug of wine, and said, smiling, "Just *vin ordinaire*. But Pouilly Fuissé would be kind of out of place here, wouldn't it?"

For a while, they chatted like the good companions they were, and Jill, watching her, was wondering, *Is something wrong? Is she holding something back?* But she kept silent and waited.

And at last Lievre said, "Roland?"

"I drove him back," Yvonne said. "I'll send his bicycle tomorrow. He's down on the road, guarding the car." She shrugged, "There's not a German soldier in the country who doesn't know that car, know also that it was a present to me from the General. If I'd left it alone, they'd have started searching the forest for me, As it is..." Another shrug. "They'll assume that Roland is one of my servants, and they won't question him at all."

Lievre nodded. "It makes sense. And what is it that brought you here?"

She sighed. "Poor Hans is in a very good mood these last two days and in the small hours of this morning I managed to find out why. You know how he likes to confide in me." There was a long pause, and then, "He knows about the attack on the camp, Lievre. He's already sending reinforcements."

Dekker felt his scalp tingling. "But...but he can't know, it's not possible! For God's sake, we made the decision only a few hours ago!"

"But..." She was frowning. "He knew of it the day before yesterday! How could that be?"

"Wait," Lievre said. "Does he know *when*? That's the important question."

"Friday the thirteenth, at twenty-three hundred hours."

The weight was dropping off Dekker's shoulders, but there was another worry now. He said slowly, "Tell me, Lievre. How many of your people knew of our original timing?"

Lievre was a step ahead of him, and he said tightly, "Seven, no more. And by God, I'll find out which one of them is a traitor!"

Yvonne Fremont was staring at them. "Your *original* timing?"

Lievre nodded. "This morning, we saw new troops arriving."

"The first contingent, without a doubt. There'll be more coming in tonight, more tomorrow night. By Friday, there'll be a very strong force waiting for you. But you've changed the schedule?"

"Tonight," Jill said. "We're going in tonight."

Yvonne breathed a sigh of relief. "Well, thank God for that! All you'll be up against tonight is a matter of seven hundred troops armed to the teeth. It's nothing, really, is it?"

"The plan we have, dear Yvonne," Hugh Black said cheerfully, "leaves me filled with the greatest confidence."

She reached out to touch him. "Good. Then we'll say no more about it."

Within moments, it was as though nothing at all untoward had happened. But Lievre said, "One thing. You're driving back to Paris alone?"

She sipped her wine. "Yes, of course. It's safe enough. No doubt, as soon as I get near the city I'll find an escort of motorcyclists; they all know my car, it's no problem."

"You'll still have to account for your absence, surely?"

"If I do, which is doubtful, I'll say I went looking for wild strawberries in the forest, the way I used to when I was a child. The little tiny ones. Poor Hans is very, very fond of them."

"In that case," Dekker said, "we'd better find you some in a hurry. I know where there's a whole bank of them, and it won't—"

He broke off when he saw her smile. She said softly, "They're in the back of the car already, Josh. I brought them from the restaurant. I'm honestly not a fool, you know."

He grinned sheepishly in embarrassment.

When the time came for her to leave, Lievre said, "I'd better find an escort for you, to see you safely back to your car," but Yvonne shook her head. "No," she said, "that won't be necessary." And Hugh Black was already on his feet, saying cheerfully, "Why don't you allow me that pleasure?"

She turned to look at him, a certain amusement in her eyes.

She was very fond of the British ex-officer, and she said, smiling, "What a shame you don't have a moustache, Major. You ought to be twirling it now."

He took her very seriously. "As a matter of fact, my dear, before we dropped, I always wore a moustache, the kind you can see the ends of from behind, a gentleman's whiskers. But Josh said it made me look too bloody British, and he made me shave it off. It's rather like losing one of your favorite bloodhounds."

She made her farewells, very affectionately, and said to Lievre, her eyes clouded with worry, "Be careful tonight, *mon cher*. The German army is fast becoming the most efficient fighting force the world has ever seen."

He nodded. "I know it, and it bothers me. Take care, my sweet."

"*Au 'voir*."

"*Au revoir*."

She took Hugh Black's proffered arm and went with him down the steep hillside, and when they were out of earshot, Jill said tightly, "On the way to the car, Josh, there'll be no trouble, if she runs into a German patrol, she holds a very privileged position. But Hugh, on the way back alone, or with only Roland..."

"Yes, you've a point there."

Del Adam said, grinning, "Mike and me, we could give them some protection."

"Okay, do that. At a distance."

"You bet," Mike 'Homer said. He was laughing openly. "The poor old Major! But they do say that middle-aged love is the best kind there is. You figure that's true?"

"Ask me in another twenty years," said Del Adam, "and I'll tell you. And you want to put down, say, ten bucks?"

"Ten bucks which says what?" Mike Homer asked.

"That he'll have her on her back before they get anywhere near the car."

"You never met an English gentleman in your life, did you, asshole? Okay, ten bucks says he won't."

As they shook hands on it, Josh Dekker said sharply, "Get with it fellas, for Christ's sake."

Still laughing, they wandered off together. It was a moment of nervous excitation that had its origins in the thoughts they both had of tonight's operation and all of its frightening dangers; there was relief in laughter.

They were both dressed in their German uniforms, masquerading as Gestapo troopers; they had no more than a dozen words of German between them.

Hugh Black was a man of extraordinary character.

He was very much a ladies' man, and yet, in his more sober moments, he reflected that ninety percent, surely, of the women he had taken to bed were professionals.

He liked to justify this by saying to himself, over and over again, "At my age, a gentleman is expected to *pay* for his pleasures, and so be it."

But in the presence of the handsome and voluptuous Yvonne Fremont, he was quite at a loss. She was not a great deal younger than he was, but whereas he showed signs of dissipation and cared very little about them, she was still young looking and fresh and beautiful, and very enticing indeed.

A bright moon filtered its rays through the treetops, and the climb down the hillside was not easy. They were within a quarter mile of the road where the car was parked, and he said; panting a little more than was necessary: "Shall we sit and rest for a while?"

She understood him at once, "Yes, let's do that. It's a marvelous evening, isn't it?"

They were talking in a mixture of French and English, each of them not very fluent in the other's language, as they found a comfortable boulder to sit on. They were holding hands, like teenagers on their first date.

"A marvelous evening indeed," he said.

"But when the moon sets..."

"Yes, that's when we're going in. It's going to be easy for us, I'm sure. But I worry about Lievre. He's mounting an attack on the eastern sector, a diversion to keep them away from us, and there are mortars there shoulder to shoulder."

"Yes, I know, but Lievre is very skillful in these things, and he knows that all he has to do is draw them away from you. All that means is, how do you say? the *appearance* of an attack. And for this, he will not lose a single man."

He fell silent for a while. And then at last he said, mumbling to hide his embarrassment, "I wish...I could wish...that your relationship with that hateful General Einstadt were not...not what we all know it is, Yvonne."

She shrugged it off. "Hateful? Yes, that's what he is, and pathetic too. I despise him, and I can't help feeling sorry for him too, sometimes."

It was a time for confidences, and she said quietly, "It wasn't entirely my own doing. He came to the restaurant; the General, three nights in a row, and I could sense his interest in me at once, even though he was very discreet about it at first. But on the third night he came very late and stayed, just sipping rather a lot of after-dinner cognac, until long after our normal closing time. We had the place almost to ourselves, and he plucked up his courage and asked me if I would consent to sleep with him. Oh, very politely, I assure you. My natural inclination, of course, was, not to tell him to go to hell, he was far too courteous about it all, but to decline just as politely. But you must realize that any senior German can get almost any woman he wants, one way or another. A few days in a dark cell with the threat of torture hanging over her, sometimes more than just the threat, and you'd be surprised how many women will take the easy way out. It happens all the time. So I asked for time to think about it, to which he instantly agreed, and I went to see Lievre."

Her hand in his was clenching and unclenching as he listened to her, and she went on. "Hans was not talking of, how do you call it, a one-night stand? He wanted me on a permanent basis, two or three times a week, and you must understand that in the Resistance we have to subjugate our own personal desires to the cause of our country, it's as simple as that. Even before I spoke with Lievre, I knew what my answer would have to be. The restaurant was already a nest of Lievre's spies, and all my waiters are bilingual. They all speak good German; they were carefully chosen because of that. There's not a single secret whispered among my German clientele that doesn't find its way to

Lievre at once. So can you imagine the advantage of a superspy in the General's own bed? And in the course of time... He's treating me now as a sort of confidante, telling me all his troubles. My God, Group 47 is the best informed group in the whole of the Resistance!"

"And still, I hate it." Hugh took both her hands and kissed them, and he said sadly, "Yes, in a war, our own feelings count for very little, don't they?"

Yvonne said deliberately, "I spread my thighs for General Hans von Einstadt, I let him do what he wants with my body, and I do what he wants with his. I betray him, and I betray myself. It doesn't make me a very honorable sort of woman, does it?"

"That, of course," Hugh Black said, "is a lot of nonsense. Surely you must know how much I adore you, admire you."

"Adore and admire me? Is that perhaps a kind of love?"

"Yes, I think it is."

"Does it mean that you want to make love with me?"

He was a little taken aback by her frankness, but he quickly recovered his senses: "Yes. It's something I've dreamed about ever since we first met." The old charm was taking over. "You remember, when we were planning the Catinat operation, you brought us our first dinner down in the cellar? You were wearing a red dress, made of very thin silk—I think it was silk."

She laughed. "Made from an American parachute!"

"You were not wearing a bra."

"I seldom do."

"And I couldn't help noticing. I was terribly excited."

"And are you excited now?"

"Yes..."

"Just looking at me?"

"Looking at you and talking with you about these things."

Her hand was on his thigh, and it crept up to his crotch and caressed him, very lightly, and she said, "You are hard, Hugh, as hard as iron. It means you want me, is it not so?"

He could hardly control himself. "Yes, it means I want you. But...perhaps this is neither the time nor the place."

"The time is always, the place is everywhere. Will it worry you that I have made myself a whore?"

"Not a whore!" he said harshly.

"Then take me now. I too have a certain feeling for you."

Her fingers were unbuttoning his fly, and she slipped her hand inside and took hold of his penis, pulling it free. She bent over and covered it with little kisses, and she looked up into his eyes and whispered, "It will be so good to make love with someone I'm fond of."

It would be a mistake, she knew, a mistake for both of them. Her present work for the Resistance made it impossible for her to allow herself the luxury of anything like falling in love, and for Hugh Black, she knew, the situation would be far worse.

How would he feel, thinking of her night after night in bed with that monster von Einstadt, the brutal and yet pathetic figure she liked to call "poor Hans," a man who could have hundreds of French hostages shot with the casual stroke of a pen? And most of all knowing the dreadful death that would be hers if her dual role were ever to be found out?

But she couldn't hold herself back now.

She took his hand and led him aside to a patch of thick and luscious ferns, with sweet-smelling honeysuckle creeping over them, and they made love there long and feverishly, exploring each others' bodies and relishing everything they found. They were both experienced and therefore expert, and it was an hour before Yvonne leaned back with a deep sigh and whispered: "My God. I must go, my love. But, we will do this again whenever the occasion presents itself. In Paris, perhaps, in my comfortable bed, where we can spend the nights together, long nights of nothing but love."

"Yes, that's what I want." He hesitated. "*Must* you sleep with von Einstadt, Yvonne? What would happen if you were to leave him?"

"If I were to leave him? There's nothing I would like more in the whole world! But the Resistance, which is more important to me than my own happiness, would lose a spy in the very highest ranks of the Gestapo. Lievre likes to tell me that I am worth fifty of his other spies, and he's right. Not one of them, good as they are, has access to secrets at such a high level! Poor Hans is—"

Hugh Black said, interrupting her: "Don't call him poor Hans, Yvonne—"

"Very well then. Damned Hans is the *head* of the Gestapo here! And he talks to me! There's never been, before, such an opportunity for us to find out their plans." She added sadly, "And if I were to leave him, who would take my place?"

"Lievre could find someone else. Another woman of high intelligence and of great beauty and sensuality, I'm sure of it! There has to be an answer, Yvonne. Because..." He was deeply moved. He said awkwardly, "This must not be a one-night stand."

"It will not be."

"It cannot be a casual meeting of lovers either, when the occasion arises. I want more than that."

"But that...that is how it *must* be, my darling."

"I loathe it."

"As I do."

They were getting nowhere. Hand in hand, they walked slowly back to where her car was parked on the road, and found Roland sitting there patiently.

"Anything?" Yvonne asked.

"Nothing," Roland said. "They took one look at the car, and they went on their way."

"Good. That's the way it's supposed to be."

The ex-Major helped her into the driver's seat as Roland got down, and Hugh took her hand and kissed it. "Let it not be too long," he whispered. "We'll be returning to Paris very soon now."

"I will be waiting. And tonight—great care, my precious. I do not want to lose you now."

He grinned at her. "It's going to be a cup of tea, I feel it in my bones."

He heard her crunch the gearshift, and watched her drive off. And he said to Roland, "Okay, let's get back to the safe-house. We've been an intolerable time. I'm afraid they'll be worried about us."

The two men moved off through the darkness of the forest.

Leutnant Mansfeld was in a furious temper.

Following on the failure of his attempt to capture Dekker and his followers, General Hans von Einstadt had summarily fired his aide-de-camp, and had transferred him to the new camp in the Gorge aux Loups, with no command mandate at all; he was to be merely the aide to the new Commandant, one Major Gerhardt Freydorf, a man who was known to have no regard whatsoever for the men in his command, not even for their lives.

He was also known for his insistence that his officers—particularly the junior ones, and more particularly those who might for the moment be in disgrace of some sort—take the most dangerous positions always, in advance of their troops so that they could lead them with exemplary courage.

And *Leutnant* Mansfeld, in his two years of military service, had almost never had occasion to fire a single shot in anger.

(The one exception was when, a few months previously, a madwoman whose husband had been executed as a hostage came at him on the Champs Elysées, brandishing a knife and screaming her poor head off. He had easily deflected the blow, knocking her to the ground and then emptying his Luger into her body, not only in anger but in great fear as well.)

And now, his damn car had broken down in the middle of the forest. It was nearly seven-thirty and he had been warned that after dark the woods were alive with members of the Resistance.

His driver said, apologetically: "I cannot fix it, Herr *Leutnant*, the differential has snapped, it needs a workshop."

Mansfeld said furiously, "I have to report to Major Freydorf by twenty hundred hours, we are already late through your incompetence!"

He struck the driver across the face with his swagger-cane, viciously, drawing blood, and he screamed: "Am I to tell him that I have an idiot for a driver? A moronic oaf? It is not an excuse the Major will easily accept! A pox on you, fool!"

There were three others with him in the disabled car. The first was his Sergeant, one *Feldwebel* Hebbel, who, before the outbreak of the war, had been a professional hunter. He had led hunting parties in the Black Forest for considerable remuneration, and he was an expert at his job. The others were two unfortunate troopers on Mansfeld's staff.

The Sergeant said diffidently, "With respect, Herr *Leutnant* we can save a great deal of time if we take a shortcut through the woods. I know the way to the camp."

"Then lead us there in haste," the Lieutenant said. "And if I am late, Sergeant, you will answer to me personally. And I do not easily tolerate inefficiency."

"We will not be late, Herr *Leurnant*," the Sergeant said quietly. "In a straight line, the camp is less than fifteen minutes march from here. And there is a track."

With *Feldwebel* Hebbel leading the way, the *Leutnant* immediately behind him, and the two troopers bringing up the rear, they set off in Indian file into the woods.

After ten minutes of carefully picking their way through the dark trees, the Sergeant stopped abruptly, and turned. He was a forest man, and in charge now, and he held a finger to his lips and whispered, his voice a zephyr, "Someone coming our way. Two men."

No more was needed. Their machine pistols at the ready, they sank down under the cover of the bushes.

Roland, whose English was very limited, had decided to speak French. He chose the simplest words, and spoke slowly and with careful clarity, because he knew that Hugh Black's French, though improving daily, was limited too. His brutish, yet amiable face was a study in animalism as he said, "How long will it take you, Major, to find that suitcase? Have you any idea?"

"We're taking Ferret with us, we hope, so it shouldn't take more than a half hour or so."

"Ah, the man Ferret. I do not trust him."

"And neither does anyone else. He's secretive, but aren't we all? We have to be. If he drops dead on us, then we'll be in the most awful trouble. And are you aware of the real reason why no one trusts him?"

"Because he appears to be a scoundrel."

"I say again, aren't we all? No. The reason is, foolishly, that he is still alive when he really ought to be dead. No one can understand how he managed to survive what he went through. It really ought not to make us suspicious of him."

"You really are a very British gentleman, aren't you?" Roland said. "But do you know the meaning of the word *naiveté?*"

"It's much the same word in English, Roland."

"Here, if we suspect, we kill. It makes much more sense. And Ferret should have been shot the moment he came to us."

"I, for one, would never have allowed it. Neither would the others. We have to take him at face value until—"

He broke off.

Out of the bushes ahead of them, no more than ten feet away, four men rose up like ghouls, their machine pistols aimed and ready, and Lieutenant Mansfeld said, in quite acceptable French, "Your hands in the air, my friends. Quite high, and immediately, *Schnell*!"

Roland raised his hands, and Hugh Black followed suit, and Mansfeld shouted: "*Soldat!* Their weapons!"

One of the two soldiers ran forward, very carefully, and removed the Anderson gun from Hugh Black's belt, the Luger from Roland's, and then stood back.

Mansfeld said abruptly, "You will come with me now. And we will find out just how resistant the men of the Resistance really are. You will keep your hands high above your heads. Lower them, and you will be cut down immediately by a burst of gunfire from four Schmeissers. Not to kill you, we need you alive. But aimed at your balls, at your knees, at your feet. *Schnell!* March!"

Then suddenly, the German Lieutenant stood there foolishly, swaying on his feet, and there was a feathered bolt protruding from dead center in his forehead, just the two-inch feathering visible.

The Sergeant had already fallen to the ground, and in a matter of five seconds or so, the two soldiers were dead, too. And Del Adam stepped out of the shadows and looked at the bodies and said, "Hey, that was pretty damn good shooting."

The little hand crossbow, powered by rubber thongs, was a weapon of enormous potency, and it was absolutely silent.

Mike Homer moved in and pulled out the bolts, because they were very valuable. They were barbed, and with his outward tugging, masses of pale-gray brain came out through the shattered forehead with them.

He looked at Hugh Black and grinned; he was a kid only just

out of college. "Shame on you, Major," he said. "You walked right into it. Christ, I could hear you two guys chattering away there a mile off, like you were in Piccadilly Circus. And believe me, this isn't London town."

"Of course," Hugh Black said apologetically, "you're absolutely right, dear boy. In a state of remarkable euphoria, for reasons which are no concern of yours, I got careless."

"No concern of mine?" Mike echoed. "You horny sonofabitch, you just lost me ten bucks."

"I did *what*?"

"Well, I guess that's no concern of *yours*. Just take it as read that Del and me...well, I gotta say, it was an education for both of us. You're quite a guy, Major."

Hugh Black was thoroughly mystified. But he'd long ago acquired the facility for not pursuing something he didn't understand, so he said brusquely, "So let's get back to the safe-house, shall we? With our loot?"

They collected four Schmeisser machine pistols for the armory of the Resistance, as well as two of the ivory-handled and quite excellent *Wehrmacht* daggers with Nazi swastikas engraved on them, and a gratifying amount of nine-millimeter ammunition; and then, they went on their way.

There were only six hours left before the assault on the camp, which had been designated Depot 32; every hour brought more and more of the reinforcements for its defense.

At twenty-two hundred hours, a German staff car drove into Depot 32, with three armored carriers in attendance. Inside were a total of nearly a hundred picked troops. It was one of the surprise inspections of which the top German brass was so fond.

The staff car flaunted the flag of a Gestapo general. And the General was no less than Hans von Einstadt himself.

CHAPTER 8

The hour was two-thirty in the morning, and there were forty-three minutes of moonlight left.

Lievre and his four hundred men had moved to within a mile of the camp, and were beginning to split up into the four groups that the leader had ordered. They were moving like foxes in the dense forest, and Lievre said quietly: "The commanders stay with me. Let's synchronize our watches. It's two-thirty-two precisely."

They set their timepieces, and moved with him to a small gully he had selected, crouching down in the damp mud at its bottom, securely hidden, close together, and huddled up like conspirators in the silence of the night.

"Everyone knows what has to be done," Lievre said, "but let's go over it all once more, and I'll answer any questions you may have. First of all, the object of the endeavor is to draw as many of the enemy as possible into the eastern extremity of the camp, while Dekker makes his assault on the western end. Except that it will not be an assault in the normal sense of the word. In German uniforms, with Ira Watslaw—whose German is better than theirs—apparently leading them, they will simply march quietly into the camp, killing the guards at the opening in the barbed-wire barricades there. Ferret is with them. He will identify the tree in which he hid his suitcase, they will recover it, and make their way back to the safe-house at once. As soon as they are well clear, they will send up one red and two green Verey lights, and that will be the signal for us to begin breaking off the battle. Now, our attack is a *diversion*, and that's all it is. This means that I want no casualties at all. The two center groups, under my direct command, will station themselves due east of the perimeter, and we will open fire at three-forty-five exactly, at a distance of fifty meters, no more. There will be forty-two mortars lined up facing us, but they can't be used at such close range. There will also be several hundred highly competent German troops in foxholes, armed with rifles, pistols, light machine-guns, and machine pistols. It means that every single man will stay under cover at all times, I don't want any idiot sticking his head out into a hail of gunfire to see what's going on. We do not have to aim, we just keep up the barrage in the general direction of the camp. The likelihood that the enemy will leave their positions is one in a million, we all know how little they like hand-to-hand combat in the dark, in the forest. No, they'll stay put. But the contingency for such an unlikely eventuality is that I will give the signal to retreat—a single red flare followed by a single white to illuminate them more than it will us. I do not expect this to happen. Any questions so far?"

One of the commanders, whose code-name was l'Ours, the Bear, asked, "The contingency. Can we assume a retreat due east? Through what would normally be a curtain of mortar fire?"

Lievre nodded. "The key word is *normally*," he said. "With their own men hard on our heels, they cannot possibly use the mortars. Which supports my argument that they will hold their positions and seek to drive us off by sheer superiority in firepower."

"And I'm a little puzzled," l'Ours said, "about the interval between your attack and mine. It seems pointless."

"No," Lievre shook his head. "We maintain our barrage for fifteen minutes. We then stop firing for seven minutes exactly, whereupon you begin on the south, and those on the north begin too. The idea is to lead them to believe that the eastern force has split up into two groups. It's a matter of confusing them. And to add to the confusion, we repeat the tactic. Seven minutes after your fifteen-minute barrage, we will open up again on the east. And by God, if this has to go on all night, it will. The runners will be bringing up fresh boxes of ammunition constantly. And I await any other questions."

No one else spoke, and Lievre nodded his satisfaction. "I repeat my warning, then," he said. "No one sticks his fool head out from behind a tree. The signal for a general retreat will simply be Dekker's one red and two green Verey lights. Once those go up, every man makes his own way home as best he can, and the operation is over. *Bon chance, mes amis*, good luck."

Quietly, the commanders moved off to rejoin their men.

Concealed by a scattering of great boulders, Dekker looked at his watch. The moon was already down, and his crew was waiting, tense and excited in the deathly silence. They were ready for any emergency, though not one of them could find fault with the plan Josh Dekker had dreamed up.

"Simplicity," he had said, "there's nothing like it if you want to deceive."

Once again, Ira Watslaw, all spit and polish, was to be their Gestapo Colonel, and Josh his Sergeant. Hugh Black, Mike Homer, and Del Adam were troopers, and Jill was dressed in khaki, the uniform of a lieutenant of the German Nursing Corps.

Save for the phony Colonel, who carried the regulation Luger 9mm pistol in its holster at his belt, and Hill, who was apparently unarmed as was correct, all of them carried Schmeisser machine pistols just like any other Gestapo troops, and all of them, without exception, had Hugh Black's favorite cyanide guns taped to their wrists, the firing clip uppermost, the tips barely protruding from the sleeves of their uniform jackets. All that was required was a sharp tap on the wrist to release a seven-foot long stream of hydrocyanic gas in short lethal bursts, five to each gun all told, each burst strong enough to ensure the almost immediate death of anyone who was unfortunate enough to breathe the merest smidgen of it.

They also carried, concealed, the eight-inch needle-pointed spikes, no thicker than chopsticks bit made of high carbon steel, which, with their oval-shaped rosewood handles, could be thrust into an enemy ear, eye, or throat, for instant and silent death. Del and Mike both carried the ordinary French cheese cutters they had grown fond of—two-foot lengths of fine steel wire with three-inch oak dowels at each end for ease of handling; they made the finest strangling cords in the world, faster than rope though far more messy, cutting cleanly through the windpipe in the first instant. And of course, they carried their Anderson guns, mostly in ankle holsters.

Ferret was dressed in the uniform of the Free French Air Force, which de Gaulle was operating out of England. His wrists had been individually bound with rope so that when he placed them together it gave the impression that they were securely fastened. He too had been given a pair of Andersons to carry under his open jacket in his belt, as well as the Commando dagger he wanted to slip in his boot.

He was thinner now than when he had first arrived; a man could not put on much weight on a diet of beef bouillon, which was all he could comfortably take, with just an occasional soft-boiled egg in mashed potatoes and milk, with a little butter to help it all on its way down. But he was moving more easily now, and his speech was almost normal, just a little hoarse. Mentally, he seemed withdrawn, and dreadfully calm, as though a moment he had been waiting for was almost on him now; as indeed, it was.

Josh Dekker said, watching him, "All right? How do you feel?"

Ferret nodded. "I'm okay." He grimaced. "I'm not the kind of man to feel very well lying on a goddamn straw paillasse day and night. I should have been up and about a long time ago." He grunted. "Maybe I'm getting old."

"It won't be long now."

"I hope not. Is that Lievre any good, Dekker?"

"The best," Dekker said.

"He doesn't impress me that much. Are you sure he's not going to chicken out at the last minute?"

"Chicken out? *Lievre?* You're crazy! I had my work cut out to stop him from what he really wanted to do, which was to mount a full-scale attack on the camp, right into the middle of it, blow everything to hell and gone! He'd have lost half of his effectives if not more. But he listens to me just once in a while. I guess that's something in his favor, too."

There was a little silence, and then Ferret said, a trifle offhandedly, "When we get my suitcase, I assume you'll hand it over to me right away?"

It was not what Josh Dekker had planned, and he said tightly, "That's a probability. But don't count on it. I'd like to know what's in it."

"I told you what's in it. My radio, and some papers."

It was not the time for a quarrel now, and Dekker pulled back. There was a very distinct possibility now, he was sure, that Ferret, a man of quite unknown qualities, just might prefer to let all that money fall into German hands rather than into Lievre's, or Dekker's own.

So he affected a sigh, and said ruefully: "Well, yes, I guess there's the question of departmental ethics here."

"You better believe it." There was a silence again, and then Ferret said softly, "Besides which, I'm the only one who can open it. It's booby-trapped."

"I figured it would be. Fulminate of mercury?"

"That's right. A hundred grams of it."

Dekker was shocked. *"A hundred grams?* Christ almighty, that's twenty times normal!"

"And much more sensible! With five grams you can blow the damn thing up under sandbags and still pick up most of what's left. But with a hundred grams, good-bye suitcase, good-bye everything in it. As well as the sandbags and anyone standing within fifty feet of it."

Yes, Dekker thought, far better to let it fall into German hands indeed.

He forced a short laugh, and said wryly, "Well, all I can say, you sonofabitch, is, this is one hell of a time to tell me. Can it explode if it's mishandled, or dropped?"

"No. Only if the locks are tampered with, or the wires under the leather are cut. And there are lots of them, crisscrossing everywhere on all six sides. Hell, you couldn't stick a needle through it without cutting a hair-wire. There are two four-digit locks, and get the numbers in the wrong order and it's a quick trip to hell, for sure."

And then (thank God! Dekker thought), a sudden eruption of furious gunfire shattered the calm of the night, a deafening barrage of enormous potency coming from the east of them, only a few hundred yards away.

It was answered almost immediately with the savage crunch of 5cm mortars, a deadly sound, all forty or more of them firing in unison and with admirable speed.

Josh Dekker looked at his watch and said calmly: "Okay, fellas, three minutes to go. Stand by."

He took a thin metal flask of cognac from his hip pocket and passed it around, a ritual with them. First Jill, then Hugh Black, then Ira Watslaw, then the two youngsters on the team, Del Adam and Mike Homer. His turn was always last, but he looked at Ferret and said slowly, "I don't know, the state your insides are in—"

"Let me be the judge of that," Ferret said, and reached for the flask.

"A sip then, don't even swallow it."

"I'm not a fool."

Josh gave him the flask, and Ferret swirled a little of it around in his mouth for a moment, and then dutifully spat it out. "What a hell of a way to drink good cognac," Ferret said.

Josh Dekker drank, and slipped the flask back into his pocket. They stood waiting in the darkness, already taking up their positions for the short march to the gates of the camp, no more than five minutes of carefully finding their way through the trees and into the semi-clearing, a generous total of eight minutes for the enemy to concentrate his forces on the east.

Josh was staring at the luminous dial of his Omega, counting the last remaining seconds.

And when the hand just touched the twelve, he said briefly, "Let's go."

When the little cortege approached the barrier, Ira Watslaw was marching briskly ahead with Sergeant Josh Dekker beside him, Ferret and Jill Magran in the center, and the three troopers bringing up the rear. They were moving quite normally, with no attempt made to hide themselves at all; everything was to be out in the open now. And the sound of the battle was fearful.

The barrier was a simple knife rest of heavy cut timbers reinforced with barbed wire and set in the space between the two extremities of the fence, and there were three guards there, an *Unteroffizier*, one *Korporal* Horscht, with two troopers.

They sprang to rigid attention at the sight of Ira's uniform, and waited, staring straight ahead like robots. Ira was frowning darkly, and he said to the corporal, "Only three men to guard the entrance to such an important site? How can that be?"

"With respect, Herr *Oberst*," the corporal said, stammering, "the others have been called to join the fighting." He was not accustomed to talking with officers above the lowly rank of *Leutnant*, and he was very nervous.

Ira stared into the darkness beyond the barrier, and he said, scowling, "And is there no guard on the equipment there? The surveyors' instruments, the machinery, the tools?"

"There...there was, Herr *Oberst*, until the firing started. But *Leutnant* Mansfeld, Herr *Oberst*, he sent a runner, Herr *Oberst*..." He broke off, sweating profusely, and said, "The Herr *Leutnant*, Sir, ordered all men from this sector of the camp, where there is really very little to guard, over to the east. For the defense, Herr *Oberst*. Just the three of us left to guard the gate."

"Very well. Then you may open it for me now."

It was a terrible moment for *Korporal* Horscht. The new camp Commandant, the fearsome Major Freydorf, had given the sentries very explicit instructions, personally. "From this moment on," he had said harshly, "all visitors to the camp will be required to show their authorization, which will be in writing, and issued only by me, over my signature, or by General von Einstadt, over his. There will be no exceptions, and any infringement of this regulation will be punished severely."

And then—the crucial comment from Freydorf: "The last Commander of this depot," the Major had said, "was brutally murdered. An intruder was seen entering Captain Haugwitz's quarters while the Captain was still alive. And he was seen leaving them after the Captain was dead. And that intruder..." There had been a dramatic pause to drive home the point, and then, "That intruder was an assassin from the Resistance, who had gained entrance by assuming the role of a Gestapo Colonel."

And now, the corporal was in a dreadful state. This Gestapo Colonel was surrounded by five others in German uniform, one of them a woman, and they had a French Air Force prisoner with them, so how could it be? Or could it?

He said stiffly, "With respect, Herr *Oberst*, my orders are to ask for your identification and authority."

"Open the barrier, fellow!" Ira said sharply. And now the Corporal knew. He was aware that three of the newcomers had broken ranks, not seeming to hurry at all, and were now much closer. In desperation, he unslung his machine pistol, and died as a single shot front Josh Dekker's silent Anderson gun drilled a hole in his skull just above the left ear. The two other men had dropped their weapons and were reaching hopelessly for the tight wires around their throats as unseen assailants behind them pulled tightly. The blood pumped furiously, spilling down onto their chests, but only for a second or two.

Hugh Black, Del Adam, and Mike Homer dragged the three dead bodies into concealment among the bushes as Josh and Ira dragged open the heavy knife rest and closed it again behind them.

"This way," Ferret said.

He led them to the giant oak trees; and stared around at the ground for a moment or two, muttering, "It's so damned dark."

Josh was getting agitated now. "What are you looking for?"

"There's a small length of stone wall, just an inch or two high, most of it buried."

"Just about here?"

"Right here, goddammit, we must be just about standing on it."

They were all on their hands and knees, groping in the darkness, brushing humus aside with their bare hands, and the minutes were ticking by. But Mike said at last, his voice a subdued whisper of triumph, "Here it is."

Ferret was beside him at once, and he crouched down and fingered the stones. His heart was beating very fast, and he nodded breathlessly. "North is...over there. Then this is the one."

He moved to a huge oak, its massive trunk only a dozen feet away. He said: "A check...there's a blaze on the trunk, but very small, I cut it with my dagger..."

"I have it," Josh Dekker said, and Ferret touched it almost lovingly. "Right. This is our tree."

He stood back and looked up into the darkness of the foliage. "About twenty-five feet off the ground, there's a major fork, two branches, both three feet or more thick, nearer to four feet. Christ, I spent the best part of the morning up there while they hunted for me. I knew they'd be back with dogs, so when they left, God, I *ran*, you won't believe how I ran."

He grunted. "Not fast enough, not far enough. Three times I crossed over water, each time I walked midstream for a couple of hundred yards or more, and still they found me. And the rest, you know."

Josh Dekker said quietly; "Del."

Del Adam slung his machine pistol over his shoulders, took one of the nylon ropes with its fist-sized anchor at one end, swung it around a few times, and sent it crashing up through the leaves. Twice, it came down again, but at the third attempt it fastened itself up there, strong and secure, and in moments Del was swarming up it, hand over hand, agile as a monkey.

And as they waited expectantly, they saw the twin blue lights of a car moving slowly in on them; over the sounds of the battle, they had not heard it. The lights were tiny pinpricks in the black-out shields over the headlamps.

Ira Watslaw said quickly, "Leave it to me, Josh. We don't want any firing at this end of the clearing, not now. It can't be an officer, not in the middle of a battle. And even if it should be, I out rank him anyway."

There was no time to take cover; the car had already stopped.

A thick and petulant sort of voice called out, "*Licht!* Lights!" and instantly an amber flood was switched on, aimed down onto the ground and bathing them all in an eerie glow. And out of the car stepped General Hans von Einstadt.

The wheels began turning rapidly in Ira Watslaw's mind, and he snapped to attention, raised his right arm, and shouted, "Heil Hitler!"

The General returned the salute with a casual wave of the hand, and an even more casual "Heil Hitler."

He said no more, but instead looked at Ira, frowning, then turned to Hugh Black and stared at him too.

A piercing look to Josh Dekker then, and at Mike Homer, and when he came to Jill he looked her up and down long and intimately.

He looked at Ferret and said, frowning, "Have I not seen this man before?"

"I think not, Herr General," Ira Watslaw said. "A French pilot who bailed out of his plane, severely damaged by anti-aircraft fire. We picked him up just three hours ago."

"Is that so?" His eyes were still on Ferret, and they were puzzled. "Come here, fellow. Let me take a look at you."

He had switched to quite fluent French, and very slowly, Ferret moved to him, his apparently bound hands held in front of him. Hardly a pace away, he stopped.

And then suddenly, with a movement as fast as lightning, he reached down into his boot for the slender Commando dagger there, swiftly drew it, and thrust it up to the hilt into the General's groin. He threw his whole weight behind the blade, and drew it up through the old man's stomach, his chest, and out at the throat.

He hurled himself aside to the ground and rolled over and over as a burst of machine pistol fire came from the car. It was answered at once by a longer burst from up in the treetop where Del Adam was. Josh, Hugh, and Mike fired their Andersons almost blindly at the car, unable to see very much, not who was there or how many there might be of them.

"Back!" Hugh Black roared, and he ran forward and sprayed cyanide gas from both his pens into the car, slapping both wrists rapidly one after the other until no more sound at all came from it.

The amber flood was still on, and Jill was crouched down beside Ferret. "Christ," she said.

He had been hit in the side and the arm, and as she tore open his clothing she said desperately, "The lower rib is hit, his arm's a bloody mess."

But the indestructible Ferret was still conscious, very much so, and as Josh bent down over him he said bitterly, "...von Einstadt, the man who had me tortured."

"Yes. I can understand it." He looked around at the others, "Anyone else hurt?"

No one was. Ira Watslaw said mildly, "We don't need that light, do we? I like the darkness better." He moved to the car, taking a long deep breath first, and wrenched out its wire. In the sudden darkness Del Adam came leaping down out of his tree; the famous suitcase was slung on a cord across his back.

Josh Dekker took it from him and said, "So let's get the hell out of here. Mike?"

"I know."

He waited for Jill to finish fixing a tourniquet on the shattered arm, and then he handed his Schmeisser to Del Adam, and picked Ferret up like a baby in his strong arms.

They strode off into the woods and up the hill, and ten minutes later Josh Dekker fired the one red and two green Verey lights that were the signal to Lievre that the mission was over.

And as they went on their way, the sounds of the battle very slowly began to die down behind them, until at last, all that was left was silence.

Ferret, still conscious and alert, said, "Dekker?"

"Yes?"

"I'll still want that suitcase from you, you sonofabitch."

"Don't talk now," Josh said. "We'll soon be home. And the poor old doc's gonna just love you for this. It kind of keeps his hand in."

The forest was closing in all around them.

CHAPTER 10

"Two million dollars in Swiss currency," Josh Dekker said glumly. "And it's all yours. Now tell me just how you're going to get your hands on it."

Lievre was even more frustrated. "Two four-digit locks, he said? That means a total of eight separate numbers, all to be set in a given sequence."

"Right."

"And without that eight-digit code, a hundred grams of fulminate?"

"Right again. That's damn nearly a quarter of a pound. Sure, it can be exploded under enough sandbags, but—"

"There'd be nothing left of the contents."

"Ashes." Dekker sighed.

"And no way Ferret's ever going to change his mind and tell us."

"Never a truer word spoken. If the Gestapo couldn't break him with what they did to him, then we sure as hell can't, even if we wanted to. And somehow, don't think we can do that to him."

"I'm tempted," Lievre said, without any conviction at all.

It was nine o'clock in the morning of the day after the battle, and they were all in the stream where Jill liked to take a bath once in a while. Hugh Black was there, and Ira and Mike and Del, all save Jill herself, splashing the cold water over their naked bodies to freshen up after the night's endeavors. Jill was in the cave with Ferret.

More sensitive than most, she admired far more than the others the tenacity and the courage that this strange—and in many ways suspicious—man had consistently shown. She had taken it upon herself to care for him as much as she could, with the doctor's help.

And as they clambered out onto the bank and sat in the sun to dry off, Gilbert, the young boy who was chief radio operator and decoder, came to them with his beloved puppy at his heels.

He held out a message for Lievre, and he said, grinning, "Hammond's on his way, our old friend Captain Hammond. He landed in England this morning at six, he's dropping in on us at twenty-one hundred hours, and will we be kind enough to put him in touch with Ferret."

"And that's from Donovan?" Lievre asked incredulously, and Gilbert nodded. "Yep. But he does say thank you and wish you luck, how about that."

"He's got his fucking nerve," Dekker said. "Why don't we just send him home again, the way we did in the Catinat operation?"

"Yes. That's exactly what we'll do, and it might teach..."

But Lievre broke off, and sat silent for a moment. He said at last, worrying it out, "No. I've got a better idea. Hammond is coming here to take over Ferret's mission, and he must know that Ferret might not be alive by the time he gets here." There was another little pause, and then, "It means he knows the combination."

Josh Dekker frowned. "Yes, but, he can't be tortured, Lievre."

"Why not, should it become necessary?"

Dekker exploded. "Jesus Christ, he's one of Donovan's boys!"

"So?" Donovan's betraying us, with Jean Moulin. I'd need a far better reason."

"Then," said Dekker, "because I won't allow it."

"Your six men," Lievre said quietly, "against my four hundred?"

Dekker sighed, and Del Adam said: "Hey, wait, I got the answer."

Josh looked at him, and Del went on, "You heard about this new idea the Gestapo came up with? You know, the one with the rags soaked in kerosene and the half-inch of candle—"

"Are you out of your mind?" Dekker said furiously, and Del raised a hand and said, "Wait, keep your fucking shirt on. I got ten bucks says he'll talk his head off long before the candle burns down."

"And if he doesn't?"

Del made an expressive gesture. "If he doesn't, then we have a guy standing by with a bucket of water, whatever. I agree, we can't let him burn the way Ferret was burned. But we can sure as hell scare the shit out of him."

"He's right, Josh," Mike Homer said. "That Hammond's a natural born chicken! Hell, we faced him down the last time, just pointing a couple of guns at him."

Hugh Black nodded. "At the very least, it's worth a try."

Dekker looked at Lievre. "What do you say?"

"I'll agree," Lievre said coldly, "on one condition."

"Which is?"

"That if it doesn't work... Then you hand him over to me."

A very worried Dekker thought about the suggestion for a long time. He said at last, heavily and not as certain as he wished he could be, "I agree with Mike, Lievre. I think Hammond's very liable to be a coward at heart. He's certainly not the stuff Ferret is made of. Okay. Let's give it a try. But first, let's have one more crack at Ferret, shall we?"

They got into their clothes, and as the others went about their business, Josh Dekker and Lievre walked back to the cave where Ferret was being tended.

He seemed to be asleep, but his eyes opened the moment the sound of their footsteps could be heard.

He was pale and drawn and very angry, his lips tight in a hard, cruel line. Jill was seated on the ground beside him, and the old doctor had found himself both a boulder to sit on and a bottle of cognac to drink from; he had decided that enough was enough and that the only solution lay in getting just a little bit smashed.

But it was Jill whom Dekker looked at, trying to understand just how deeply she felt for this man. "How is he?" he asked.

She rose to her feet to stretch her cramped legs. "His heartbeat is strong, and so is his pulse."

"Don't forget the mind," Ferret said sourly, "my mind is strong too."

115

"Yes, the mind," the old doctor said, his voice a little slurred. "And that's the most important organ in the body, did you know that?"

Dekker grunted. "The power of positive thinking? Is that what you're talking about?"

"Yes, I suppose it is, just that. But I must ask myself what more they can do to him before he just...just lies down and dies."

Jill said gently to the wounded man, "Would you like some more soup? It just needs warming up."

He shook his head. "Not till I find out what it is these gentlemen want. As if I didn't already know."

"We thought," Josh said carefully, "that on more mature reflection you might have decided to give us the combination and be done with it. It's the only sensible thing now."

"I will not. Instead, I will remind you of what you called departmental ethics. It's a nice phrase, isn't it? Though it doesn't seem to mean a hell of a lot to you."

"Listen," Lievre said, losing his limited patience, "we know what's in that suitcase, and we know where it's supposed to be going."

Ferret seemed almost to smile. "I doubt that," he said, and Dekker answered, "Two million dollars in Swiss Francs for Jean Moulin's *Combat*."

"Ha! If that's what you think...then it explains everything, doesn't it? Though I can't help wondering where you picked up a story like that."

"Certain sources in Cairo, sources that have always proved reliable."

"This time, I'm afraid you've been grossly misinformed. Whatever money there is there, it is *not* for Jean Moulin."

"A lie!" Lievre said angrily.

But Ferret looked at Josh and said quietly, "I give you my word of honor. I'll swear to it on my mother's grave, on a stack of bibles if you can find them, even though I feel that my word ought to be enough. That money is *not* for Jean Moulin, nor for any other Resistance leader."

"Then where's it going?"

Ferret shook his head. "I'm not at liberty to tell you. I might even feel I should say I'm sorry I can't, but, we're back to those ethics, aren't we?"

"We're wasting our time," Lievre said furiously. "We have to find another way to open it, that's all there is to it."

He stalked out of the cave, and Josh Dekker said, "Come with us, Jill."

"All right." She turned to the doctor. "He ought to take some more food soon, I think."

"Very well." The doctor put his bottle away and stood up. "I'll see to it."

They found Lievre waiting for them some distance from the cave, and Dekker said brusquely: "Hammond, he's our only hope now."

"Agreed," Lievre said. "Only, one thing."

"Which is?"

"This has to be *my* operation. Donovan has asked *me* for a reception committee, and if Hammond sees you, or any of your people with me, he might just smell a rat. We don't know how devious a man he is, how suspicious, how clever. All we know about him is that he most probably doesn't have Ferret's kind of courage. So, I don't want him to think there's someone who'll maybe come to his rescue at the last moment. That means you have to keep out of sight during the drop."

Dekker scowled. "I told you, Lievre, I fully support your claim to that money. You don't have to cut me out of the operation, I'm on your side, for Christ's sake!"

Jill said quickly, "He's right. We've no way at all of guessing at Hammond's intelligence, and fellow Americans standing around, he wouldn't believe it, Josh!"

"Okay, okay, perhaps you're right at that. What time's he arriving?"

"Twenty-one hundred hours."

"Okay. I'll keep the fellas out of your way."

Lievre smiled thinly. "If it makes you feel any better, you get to take care of the suitcase while all this is going on."

"Yeah. I'll do that."

And so, it was decided. Captain Hammond was going to have the shit scared out of him, in the hope that he'd turn chicken before he really got hurt.

The moon was partly obscured by clouds as they set up the tiny fires for the letter of the day. The clearing was no more than fifty feet across. And at two minutes to nine at night they heard the ack-ack fire not very far to the north of them, saw the shells exploding up there, and the bright beams of the searchlights. And moments later, there was the plane itself, a British Dakota gliding in at reduced speed, at no more than six hundred feet. As it passed directly overhead, the pilot gunned his engines and the plane disappeared swiftly from their sight, still followed by a barrage of bursting shells.

Soon, they saw the two parachutes, and in seconds, Captain Hammond hit the ground and collapsed his 'chute. He slapped the buckle of his harness and ran quickly to where his container had landed—a metal cylinder some three feet long and eighteen inches across. As he began unfastening its cords, he saw that a dozen or more men were approaching him, led by the man named Lievre, whom he had met once before.

He straightened up and said, amiably enough, "Captain Julius Hammond, Lievre, code-named Sandman. And I hope the circumstances of this meeting will be better than those of the last one. I've come to take over from Ferret, as I'm sure you know. Is he still alive?"

"He is."

"And his suitcase?"

"We're taking very good care of it," Lievre said blandly.

"Good. And Dekker?"

"Dekker? Oh, he's not here. They left early this morning for St. Lô. Something to do with Jill Magran's grandparents, who live there. It seems the Germans have somehow found out Mademoiselle Magran's origins, so her family's in danger."

"Good," Hammond said again. "I never did like that man, he's a troublemaker."

But Lievre was staring at the Captain's clothing; he was in the uniform of an American airman. Hammond said, smiling broadly, "Is it my dress that puzzles you? My French clothing is in the container there, with my radio stuff. I figured there was always a chance of being dropped to the Jerries the way Ferret was. I had no wish to be captured out of uniform." He tapped his head. "A wise man thinks about these things."

So, Lievre thought, *a coward indeed*. It was good news.

"Well," he said brusquely, "be that as it may, I'm afraid you must consider yourself my prisoner, Captain."

Hammond's mouth dropped open. "Say again..."

"My prisoner." He gestured. "Roland."

Roland ran forward and quickly relieved Hammond of his automatic and his ammunition as the Captain held his hands high in the air; there were a dozen assorted guns leveled at him, very steadily.

He said angrily, "But...for God's sake! Why? What the hell for? Are you out of your mind? I'm one of Donovan's men!"

"If you can't shut up," Lievre said coldly, "at least keep your voice down. There are Germans all around us. What we have planned for you is rough, but it's nothing compared with what the Gestapo's capable of."

The Captain's voice was hoarse, and the blood had drained from his face. "'*Planned for me?*' I don't understand."

"It's very simple. We need the combination to Ferret's suitcase, which you must know. All you have to do...is give it to us."

"Over my dead body," Hammond said tightly, and Lievre nodded:

"Yes," he said mildly, "that's indeed a possibility we've reckoned with."

The Captain fell silent as 'Roland bound his hands behind his back. And in a moment, trembling with rage and with fear too, he was prodded with a machine pistol in the small of his back, out of the clearing and into the woods.

As the little group found its silent way back to the safe-house, Roland was bringing up the rear, carrying the container and the two bundled-up 'chutes. Parachute silk was highly prized by the women of Paris, and worth its weight in gold.

Hammond, stripped naked, lay on a fallen tree trunk, his legs straddling the trunk with his feet tied underneath it. There was a rope holding his neck down, and his hands were tied to the trunk above his head. The kerosene-soaked rags, a wet pile of them between his thighs, were burning him, though not intolerably so. Not yet, he thought. He was trembling more furiously now, scared out of his wits, even more so when he saw Roland, grinning like a devil, leaning over to balance a candle precariously on top of the rags. It was just a stub no more than an inch long. Hammond thought he had never seen a more brutish face in all his life.

"Better you don't try to move none," Roland said in broken English. "That *chandelle* fall over, burn down, *pouff*. Nice little fire keep you warm. Only soon, you don't got no balls left."

"When the time comes," Lievre said clearly, "when you finally come to your senses, all you have to do is call out '*Vive la Résistance*.' It will mean you are ready to give us the combination. We will be close enough to hear you."

As they melted into the darkness of the trees around them, Roland said quietly, "Dekker said something about a bucket of water, for when the flame gets too low?"

Lievre said coldly, "No. If he doesn't want to talk, then we've lost out. And we'll have no further use for him."

They peered through the foliage at the naked man bound there. And even at this distance, in the faint light of the clouded moon, they could see the sweat pouring down from his forehead as he lay deathly still.

The only sound to break the heavy silence was the plaintive cry of an owl.

For more than an hour, Captain Hammond just lay there. His head had been propped up with a small log for a pillow, so that he could easily watch the flame that signaled the approach of the most dreadful agony his feverish mind could imagine. And it was his mind that was being tortured now, as he desperately tried to think of the *good* life that had been his before that reckless maniac Wild Bill Donovan had laid all that bullshit on him about serving his country.

And it *had* been a good life. His father was the famous Victor

Todd Hammond who had been political advisor to Jake Dickenson of Tennessee, the Secretary of War in the Taft Administration. This had meant, when Julius was just a kid, travels to Paris, Rome, and the Berlin of the old days, followed by places like Athens, Bucharest, Belgrade, and finally Tirana, further and further down the scale as the old man took to hitting the bottle rather more than Washington found necessary.

Even so, after his parents' quite nasty divorce, this was glamour in its most exotic form for the obnoxious youngster. He cordially hated his father, and stayed with him just because of the money. Victor Hammond was impossibly rich, and had contrived to keep almost all of his wealth out of the hands of the nagging ex-wife whom he thought of only as a goddamn pest.

The flame of the candle was impossibly low, flickering in a nonexistent breeze; a fold of the soaked rags was perilously close. Would it be a sudden burst of rapid fire? No, the smell, very strong, told him that it was kerosene, not gas. It would begin by smoldering and then flames would begin.

He thought of the women he'd known, so very many of them. With his youthful good looks, his ease with languages, his elegance, and especially all of that cash poured into his pockets by a father who just wanted the damn kid out of his hair, women were a dime a dozen for him. They were young or cider, blonde or brunette, rich or poor, beginners or pros; just like Don Giovanni, he used to keep a list.

There'd been the cars too, he was crazy about cars. There was the red Maserati his dad had given him for his eighteenth birthday, the Model A Ford with the big Chrysler mill he'd put into it, plus the beautiful 11-liter Hispano-Suiza he'd bought for himself (it cost some forty thousand dollars even in those days), which he used when he really wanted to impress one of his ladyloves.

He found he couldn't take his eyes off that steady yellow flame; a corner of the rag was beginning to smolder now.

He thought of the nightclubs and the cocktail bars where he was so well known, hundreds of them in a dozen different cities, of the Windmill Theater and the Folies Begere, of the casinos in the south of France, of splendid meals in four-star restaurants, and of his women again.

121

And for God's sake, he was giving all this up for the sake of heroics?

He smelled the cloth just beginning to burn, and he shouted, not really thinking about it, *"Vive la Résistance!"*

Lievre and some of the others were beside him at once, and Lievre said tightly, "You are sure?"

"Yes, I'm sure, for Christ's sake! One three five seven, two four six eight!"

"It's not an attempt to blow us all up? Yourself included?"

"No, no, *no!*"

Lievre said sardonically, "I believe you, Hammond. You're not the suicidal type, are you?"

He swept the candle and the rags away and said roughly, "But just to make sure, you'll open the case yourself, with no one else less than a dozen meters away."

Roland unfastened the ropes, and Lievre went on, "Get dressed. You'll come with us now. Once the case is safely opened, you'll be free to move around a little, but always in your French airman's uniform. Believe me, you won't last long in this part of the world dressed like that if you try to leave our camp."

"And then?" Hammond had lost every vestige of his fear, and hardly a trace of conscience had taken its place.

Lievre shrugged. "We have no personal grudge against you, Captain Hammond. We'll send you home." He added maliciously; "As we did once before, I remember."

A soft rain began as they moved off in the darkness.

CHAPTER 11

Under the watchful eye of an outraged Ferret, the money was being counted and transferred from the now-open suitcase into canvas sacks.

They were all in the cave—Dekker, Hugh, Ira, Del, and Mike, with Jill watching over the wounded man, still worried about him. Lievre was there too, and the old doctor, and a dozen of the men of the Resistance; it was a good day for them all, save for Ferret.

He was still in ignorance of Hammond's arrival, and he said to Josh Dekker, trying to keep the anger from his voice, "As one agent to another, I don't suppose you want to tell me how you got that case open? It's supposed to be foolproof."

"Well," Josh said nonchalantly, "it's academic now, isn't it? Let's say we found a way to do it, and leave it at that."

But Lievre was not so sympathetic, and he said, as though it had nothing to do with the matter in hand, "Did I tell you that Captain Hammond is here? No, I don't believe I did, it must have slipped my mind."

"Hammond?" Ferret scowled. "What the hell's that asshole doing here? He's supposed to be some place in Tunisia."

"He's come to take over your mission," Lievre said vengefully. "At least, that's what he was hoping to do."

Ferret stared at him openmouthed. He turned to Dekker and said incredulously: "You mean *Donovan* sent him?"

Dekker nodded. "He thought that maybe you were dead. Seems like someone dropped a hint to that effect."

"You bastard. Just tell me how many fingernails he lost before

123

he told you?"

"He wasn't hurt, he just ran scared."

"It figures. And what happens now?"

Lievre rejoined the discussion, tossing the last of the currency bundles into the last of the sacks. "I'm sending you both to London," he said. "We've already asked for a light plane to come and pick you up."

For a long time, Ferret said nothing. Jill reached out to touch him, and she said gently, "It's the best thing for you now. Within twenty-four hours or so, you'll be in a good hospital bed, with some of the finest doctors in the world to look after you."

He took her hand and clenched it, and he said clearly, "Jill, you're the only friend I've found here, and I thank you for it. But no. I don't want to go to London. I won't impose on you too much, but my mission is over now, aborted." He hesitated. Then, very quietly to her, "Can you persuade your friends to send me to Paris?"

He turned to Dekker when she didn't immediately answer him, and he said roughly, "I'm not the kind of man who often begs, but...will you get me to Paris?"

Josh looked at Lievre, not quite sure. "What do you think? As he says, his mission's been aborted, he can't harm us, and...well, I don't know."

"He has to go to London," Jill said desperately. "If his life can be saved at all, it has to be in England! There's not a hospital in Paris that will take him in his condition, they know the Gestapo would find out in no time at all, he'd be back in their cellars again! Is that what you want?"

"Wait, wait," the always-suspicious Lievre said.

He looked at Ferret. "Just tell me what there is in Paris for you."

"A girl," Ferret said. "Just...a girl."

"Oh."

"It's doctors you need now, for God's sake!" Jill said. "Not women!"

"She'll know what to do," Ferret said stubbornly. "I'll be in good hands, and out of your hair. And you'll never see me, nor hear from me again."

It seemed that the silence would never end. At last, Hugh Black said quietly, "When are we going back to the old safe-house, Josh? To Yvonne's place?"

"Any day now; our work here's finished."

"Then we should take him with us. Get him to his girl, and that's an end to it. Ira? What do you think?"

Ira Watslaw nodded vigorously. "I for one have no wish to see him manhandled aboard that plane against his will. After all, we just stole two million Swiss francs from him, so maybe we owe him something. And there's not a man among us who doesn't admire his guts. Yes, let's do that."

Dekker turned to Lievre. "Okay? Can you warn Yvonne in time?"

"Yes, I'll send Roland, right away. And as soon as the curfew's lifted in the morning, I'll get the truck to take him back."

"Good." Josh turned to Del and Mike, the inseparables, "Ready at first light, fellas."

"You bet," Del Adam said. "I don't know about you guys, but I've been ready ever since the first minute we got here. Haven't had a decent meal since then, I just can't wait for some of Yvonne Fremont's cooking."

Hugh Black stared down at Ferret and said, a twisted smile on his face, "I haven't really had a chance to say this before, my friend, but, your unexpected killing of the General, I want to thank you for it."

"Huh?"

"For reasons of my own, dear boy, I was almost ready to do it myself."

"And this girl of yours," Dekker asked. "Where does she live?"

"Number twenty-one Quai de l'Horloge, up on the third floor. You can see Notre Dame from her bedroom window."

"And her name?"

Ferret hesitated. He sighed. "Yes, I suppose you have to know it, don't you? It's Simone Delaunay."

"A description too, just in case of accidents."

"She's thirty-two years old, long dark hair, dark eyes, quite pretty, weighs about a hundred and five I think."

125

"And her code-name?" Lievre asked, not being very subtle about it.

But Ferret shook his head. "No, she's not in the Resistance."

"Her occupation?"

"Shopping," Ferret said drily. "They have enough money. More correctly, her husband has money."

Lievre's dark eyebrows shot up. "Her *husband?*"

"Yes, her husband. And it gets worse, I'm afraid. He's a wine merchant, and his best customer these days is the German Army. He's very, very friendly with a number of their senior officers."

"And she is too?" Lievre's voice was very harsh, but Ferret said emphatically, "She hates *them* as much as she hates *him*. It's not exactly an ideal marriage."

He saw that neither of them was very happy, and he went on, speaking very quickly now, "Ever since I first went to the States twelve years ago, I've been making twice-yearly trips to Europe, sometimes three or even more times a year. I first met her seven years ago, and we've been...friends ever since. She's absolutely trustworthy, if that's what's worrying you. I'd trust her with my life, which is what I'm doing now."

"Then you can hardly stay in her apartment."

"Of course not! We'll find somewhere. Don't worry, for Christ's sake! She is a one-hundred-percent French patriot, and a secret Gaullist. Secret, that is to say, from her husband Jacques, all her close friends know how she feels."

Mike Homer said lightly, "Ferret, Hammond, and now Simone Delaunay. Life's getting kind of complicated, isn't it?"

An hour after sunup the following morning, a rattletrap old produce truck loaded with potatoes for the city was waiting for them on a side road below the hideout, its hood thrown open and a driver hard at work on the engine, doing nothing, to simulate a breakdown.

It was the same truck that had carried them from the dropping ground to Paris on their first arrival in France, when they were working for Donovan and had not yet recovered from the enthusiasm with which he had inspired them. The *bullshit*, they called it now.

Mechanically, it was always kept in first-rate condition, its body work was held in place here and there with baling wire. They avoided the constant danger of being commandeered by the German Army by giving the impression that the truck was a wreck.

Below the truck's bed, at the back, there was a plank some eighteen inches wide that could be removed to disclose a hidden compartment under the bed, running its full length and width, a hiding place for black market meat that could be smuggled to a few selected restaurants. It was not the most comfortable hiding place in the world, but as many as nine or ten men had, on occasion, been squeezed in there, lying on their backs and scarcely able to move a muscle in the claustrophobic (and very smelly) darkness. There was a tiny red light down there which meant, when it was switched on, that danger was looming—a roadblock or prospective search, whatever.

Josh groaned when he saw it. "Christ," he said, "I'd hoped we'd outgrown that damn thing." Lievre answered cheerfully, "You have. But what about Ferret? A badly wounded man up there in the back? Wouldn't that be asking for trouble?"

"True enough."

They had long since acquired false identity papers, but except for Jill and Ira there was the pressing problem of language, and they elected to ride all together and share the discomfort. Ferret was slid carefully in first, then Jill to lie on one side of him and Josh on the other, with the rest of them slithering in as best they could.

"I'll be in Paris in a few days," Lievre said. "Till then, *bon voyage, mes amis.*"

A few moments later, the old truck was rattling off over the bomb-scarred roads of the forest and out onto Route N-7 which would take them past the Gorges d'Apremont on the one side and the rocks of Cuvier-Chatillon on the other, through the little town of Chailly-en-Biere, and on to Paris.

Three times, the little red light went on, and they held their breath as they listened to the sounds of the guards at the roadblocks, felt the rocking of the truck as sacks of potatoes were thrown around for a cursory search. But part of the load was for the German garrison at Les Invalides, and the delay was slight.

And just after ten o'clock in the morning, they pulled into the tiny delivery yard of the restaurant called le Cochon Qui Rit, The Laughing Pig, and the tall timber gates were closed behind them.

Madame Yvonne Fremont, warned by Roland, was there herself to greet them as they crawled one by one out of their confinement, cramped and bruised but glad to be home again. She embraced them all warmly, especially Hugh Black, and she said, "Quickly, please, there's a lot of activity on the street, more patrols than I've seen in a long time."

She looked at Ferret, almost out on his feet and held up by Del Adam, and said gravely, "You are welcome here, M'sieur, and you will be safe here too, I promise you. And I've arranged for a doctor, an excellent doctor, to come by this afternoon."

"You are most kind, Madame," Ferret whispered painfully.

"Come, follow me."

She led them through a thick and heavy wooden door and down a twisting flight of steps into the beginnings of the vast wine cellars, lined with racks filled with dusty bottles on three walls. Five huge barrels on their sides took up the fourth wall; each one was some six feet across, each with its own wooden spigot and a *tâte-vin*, a silver tasting saucer, hanging beside it. She went to the third barrel, and turned its end around ninety degrees, pulling it free as it came apart. The barrel was a tunnel that led into a subsidiary cellar with whitewashed walls and a timbered ceiling, lit by a dozen bare bulbs.

She looked at Hugh and smiled, "And it's good to see you, all of you, home again."

He held her hands, delighted, and as he looked around the room he saw that everything had been done that was necessary; their sleeping bags (easier to hide than cots in case of an emergency) had been neatly stacked in a corner, and Hugh's own box of tricks was there. There was a bottle of Augiers Frères cognac on a table with half-a-dozen bottles of Château Neuf du Pape and glasses, and all the plates and cutlery they had been using before. It was indeed a very pleasing homecoming.

But it was apparent that Ferret's condition had greatly deteriorated. He lay on the canvas cot that Yvonne brought for him with his arms tightly clasped over his stomach, as though to stifle the awful pain they knew he must be suffering. He was paler than they had ever seen him before, weaker even than when they had found him trussed in that dreadful torture chamber; from time to time his eyes seemed to be glazing over as though he might lapse into a coma at any minute.

But he was still mentally aware of what was going on, and he whispered, breathing heavily, "The girl...Simone...she will know where to take me. This...this will pass, I promise you."

But then the doctor arrived, a young and very bright medical student from Sorbonne University. He listened in silence, shaking his head from time to time as Josh told him what had happened, the burned genitals, the electric shocks down into the intestines, all the rest of the horror. And he said at last, very firmly, "A hospital. He needs considerable surgery. There is no other way."

He was in shock himself. As a longtime member of Group 47 of the Resistance, he had seen his share of torture victims, but most of them had been corpses by the time he'd gotten to them.

"I will not...will not...go to a French hospital," Ferret said clearly, and the young doctor agreed at once. "Of course not," he said. "And even if I could find the skilled surgeon you need, how can we operate here?"

He turned to Dekker. "Surely there must be a way of getting him to London?"

There was still time to take him, at considerable risk, to the hidden airstrip where Hammond's plane would be, but Ferret was still adamant. It seemed as though the strength of his obstinacy had somehow transposed itself to his shattered body when he said, with almost a wry grin on his face, "The *mind*, Dekker! Remember the words of that wise old man in the cave, 'the mind is the most important organ in the body.' Believe me, he was right! Just...just get the girl, and she'll know where to take me. I refuse to go to London now."

The doctor threw up his hands. "All I can do, then," he said, turning to Yvonne, "is sedate him, and give him an analgesic, it will help."

"Good," Dekker said, "then do that, please."

Out came the hypodermics from the little leather bag, and in a very few moments Ferret relaxed his cramped position and murmured, "It's like...like a cheap...a cheap drink, isn't it?"

"He'll be asleep very soon now," the doctor said. "Just let him rest, and we'll all just *hope*. And if you need me again, Yvonne, you know where to find me."

When he had gone on his way, a very vital question arose—the question of the girl.

"We can't take him to her place," Dekker said, "and run the risk of meeting her husband, obviously. And yet, how can we bring her here? To the safest safe-house in Paris? A woman we know nothing about except that she almost certainly works for Jean Moulin?"

"My car, then," Yvonne said, "and a blindfold. The phone's in my office, Jill."

"Okay."

As they moved to the barrel entrance of the hideaway, Yvonne turned back and said to Hugh Black, very calmly and as though it were the most natural thing in the world, "Why don't you come with us, Hugh? I have to show you where my private quarters are. You've never seen them, have you?"

He was startled. "Your private quarters?"

"Roland told me about...poor Hans. You have to know where my bedroom is. Come."

He looked at the others, Josh Dekker and Ira Watslaw carefully avoiding his eyes, Del and Mike grinning at him broadly; with only the briefest hesitation he sheepishly followed the women out.

The office was a delight.

It was quite small, and its walls were mostly covered with menus from the city's older and finer restaurants—Foyot, Larue, Tour d'Argent, Voisin, Drouant, and others, many of them long gone now. There was a splendid canvas of Yvonne herself, painted twenty years previously when she had been a bare-breasted *danseuse* at the Folies Begere, and two good paintings of the kind sold by artists in their outdoor studios in Montmartre. There was a divan along half of one wall covered in pale green silk, a single matching armchair, a desk of polished walnut, two wooden chairs, and a very small sideboard on which stood several bottles of wine and a half-dozen crystal glasses.

Yvonne opened a drawer and found the phone book, and as Jill looked up the number, she poured three glasses of her favorite Château Neuf du Pape for them all.

She watched Jill dialing, then caught Hugh's look and smiled; she raised her glass and said softly, "To us, my darling."

"Yes, to all of us."

Jill said politely into the phone, "May I please speak with Madame Delaunay?"

It was a man's voice that answered, brusque and a little uncouth, from Marseilles, by his accent.

"Who's this?"

"The dressmaker, M'sieur."

"Hold the line."

And then, in a moment, the more cultured voice of a woman, the accent pure Parisian, "Elaine? I didn't expect to hear from you so soon."

Jill said quickly, "Try not to show surprise, Simone. I've come from Ferret."

There was no immediate answer, and Jill suddenly thought, "Oh, God, she doesn't know his code-name..." It had not occurred to her before, and she worried about it. But then Simone was there again, playing her part very nicely. "Oh. I can't wait to see them," she said delightedly. "What colors did you get?"

"I'll be waiting for you at the north end of the Pont des Arts," Jill said. "You don't normally rush off to see your dressmaker, I imagine, so take your time. I'll be there in fifteen minutes, and I'll wait all day if necessary. I'm wearing a green blouse and a gray skirt, with high-heeled, dark green shoes. And my name..." She hesitated. "My name is Defarge."

It was the code-name given her long ago by Alphonse, who called himself le Lievre, the Hare, more as a kind of sardonic joke than anything else. She seldom used it, and had almost forgotten it.

The voice on the phone was saying casually, "I think the blue is probably the one I want, but I'd like to see them all. I'll come over just as soon as I can, in half an hour or so. And thank you for calling, Elaine."

Jill put down the phone and sat still for a moment, frowning. She said at last, looking at Yvonne, "And why is it that something is

131

worrying me? Something I can't put my finger on?"

"About Simone?"

"Yes. But I suppose I'll find out when I meet with her."

She took the car keys from Yvonne and left them, and Hugh Black said slowly, "I think I know what's worrying her, it's been worrying me, too. According to Ferret, Simone has no code-name. But if she's working with him, as Josh suggested..." He thought about it for a moment. "I'll go a step further, Yvonne. Since Ferret came here to meet with Jean Moulin, I find it pretty apparent that Simone is his contact here, working with *Combat* too. She's the girl who's going to take him to Moulin, a man who moves around so fast and so carefully that he's very, very hard to find. But surely, *someone* must know where he is at all times, no?"

"Yes, I'd say so."

"Don't worry too much," Yvonne said, "that Ferret wouldn't give us a code-name for her, most of the Resistance groups keep their code-names secret from each other, as we do. And in any case, Ferret's been lying from the very beginning, hasn't he? Nothing but lies, lies, lies. But what worries me is, why does he want to continue with his mission when he's lost the money? *That* is the question, Hugh."

"It's a mystery."

"And I don't particularly care for mysteries. In the life we lead, they can sometimes be very dangerous."

She shrugged. "But Jill will find out. You don't know what a treasure that girl is. And meanwhile..."

She took his glass from him and placed it on the sideboard beside her own, and threw her arms around his neck, kissing him furiously.

"And meanwhile," she said, "we have just a little time to wait for Jill's return, so let's not waste it."

She took his arm and led him to the door. "Let me show you my bedroom, we'll be much more comfortable there."

CHAPTER 12

Jill knew who it was the moment Simone came to the north end of the Pont des Arts; there was something in the urgency of the step, the very visible excitement, that made her absolutely sure.

She was a woman of obviously expensive tastes, dressed in a smartly tailored suit of burgundy colored wool with a ruffled white silk blouse. She was carrying a beige leather purse on a strap over her shoulder, a purse that was far too large and seemed somehow out of place. Her hair was dark and thick and fashionably set, and her hazel eyes were just a trifle slanted and very large and sensual. She seemed to wear almost no makeup at all, and Ferret's description of her as quite pretty was a gross understatement, the kind of description that could come only from a very sardonic man at his most disparaging.

She almost ran across the road, ignoring the angry beeps of heavy traffic and the screech of sudden braking, and went straight into the beautiful gardens of the Louvre, with their bright geraniums and anemones and carefully manicured lawns.

She saw the green blouse and gray skit at once, but she affected not to notice them. Instead, she began sauntering quite slowly, made as if to walk right by Jill, and as she passed her, she murmured, "Defarge?"

"Yes," Jill said, "I'm Defarge. Simone?"

"Of course." She turned back at once and faced Jill. "Where is he?"

"In a safe place. I'm here to take you to him."

"And you? What have you to do with him?"

"I'm helping him."

133

"He never told me he'd need help from anyone but me."

"The circumstances demanded it," Jill said. Simone now began what she thought of as very cautious questioning indeed. It did not faze her in the least; Paris these days was a place where carelessness could lead to rapid extinction at the hands of the most ruthlessly repressive and brutal force in modern history.

The wheels were turning very fast in Jill's head as she weighed her answers with the greatest circumspection; she too had learned the need for watchfulness.

"You are in the Resistance, no doubt," Simone said. "Which group?"

Jill shook her head. "I'm not, as a matter of fact. I sometimes work for a man code-named Lievre, but I'm not a member of his group, nor of any other."

"I've heard of him; they say he's next in importance only to Jean Moulin."

"Both of them are ardent patriots and fine soldiers for France."

"What do you do for him?"

"I solve problems."

"What kind of problems?"

"Like this one, for example," Jill said smoothly. "When Ferret told me of the difficulty he might have in reaching you, or even in calling you at the apartment, because of your husband, you understand, I suggested that I take you to him instead."

"How did he find you in the first place?"

"Lievre sent me to him, for this specific purpose."

"And does Ferret pay you?"

"Of course." (Was it the right answer? she wondered.)

"A great deal of money?"

Jill answered with a shrug, "Enough. I'm not here to discuss my financial arrangements."

"How can I be sure you're not from the police?"

"That's very simple. Ask me questions the police would not be able to answer."

"Very well."

Simone took a long, deep breath, and then asked, "His real name, he must have told you that."

"Actually, he should not have done, but he did. I told him it was very bad security, but he just laughed, you know how he is."

"And the name?"

"Miles Foresome."

"You know how he came here?"

"A parachute drop in the forest of Fountainebleau. To a reception committee of the Resistance arranged by Lievre."

"The name of his boss?"

"Colonel Donovan."

"Where?"

"In Cairo."

Then, the clincher, "The amount of money."

"Two million Swiss francs," Jill said clearly, and Simone smiled.

"Well," she said, "that seems to settle it. *Bien*, take me to him."

"Not so fast," Jill said, and it was her turn now to find out a great deal that she wanted to know. "I commend you for your caution, but I'm cautious too, both by nature and from experience. How can I be sure that you really are Simone Delaunay, and not someone sent by your husband and his German friends? Ferret never described you very well, he merely gave me your phone number."

"Oh for God's sake."

There was a certain anger in those splendid eyes now, and Simone said irritably, "You called me, and I came. Isn't that enough?"

"No, it is not."

The sudden anger gave Jill an advantage, she thought, and she pushed it home at once, saying carefully, "I have to be sure, Simone. So...only Ferret and I and Simone Delaunay know of his plan. Just tell me the first step."

Simone threw up her hands in eloquent disgust.

"The first step," she said patiently, "is, we drive in my car all the way to Strasbourg to meet with one of his old business partners, whose name I do not know, he never told me. He will have all the necessary forged papers for us, the papers we'll need to cross the border."

"I find it surprising that you don't know his name," Jill said, trying to get just a little further along. Simone said, with an air of

135

desperation, "Miles never told me that! All I know about this man is that he's coming from Geneva, to get us over the border without any hassle. Wait!"

It is an inspiration, and she was digging into her oversized purse. "If that isn't enough for you—there, my passport, that should convince you, unless you're going to pretend it's a forgery."

As she handed it over, Jill said mildly, "There aren't many people who carry their passports around with them all the time." No sense in giving up too easily!

But Simone said, more calmly now, "I don't. I have it with me now, for good reason."

Jill looked at the unflattering photo, at the date and place of birth, and as she gave it back she smiled and said, "Forgive me, Simone. But this is a very risky business, as you must know."

"Sure, Will you take me to him now?"

"My car's parked just off rue St. Honore, at the B.P."

"And then, can we leave at once?"

Jill pulled up short. "Won't you have to return home first?"

"For what? There's nothing there for me now."

"Well, to pack a bag? You'll need some clothes, surely?"

"I have no intention," Simone said deliberately, "of ever returning to that loathsome apartment, nor to my equally loathsome husband. He treats me abominably, he's a Fascist and pro-German, he's looking for a post of authority in the *Milice* when it gets moving, and I hate him! No! Ferret is a *release* for me, from something I've suffered far too long, and the sooner we can move, the better I'll like it. Why do you think I brought my passport with me?"

She laughed suddenly, "And I assure you, my dear, that with two million Swiss francs to live on, we can manage very nicely indeed for a very long time. They do have good dressmakers in Switzerland too, you know. So let's be on our way, and farewell Paris forever!"

As they walked together up rue du Louvre and onto rue de Rivoli, Jill was deep in thought, and she said at last, very quietly, "You'd better know now, Simone, before you see him. Ferret's been quite badly hurt."

Simone stared at her. "Oh, God—how badly?"

"Badly enough, I'm afraid. There were times when it seemed

certain he wouldn't live, times when an ordinary man would have just...given up and died. But he's not ordinary, is he?"

"No, he's not. And is that why he came so late? What happened?"

As gently as she could, Jill told her as much as she thought was desirable, and Simone's face grew paler by the minute; she was dabbing at her eyes with a handkerchief from time to time as she listened. But she took hold of herself by a strong effort of will, and she said, "I was a nurse once, did he tell you that?"

"No."

"It was before I married that monster Jacques, but I haven't forgotten everything I learned."

"He did say you could look after him. But he'll need surgery, Simone, quite urgently."

"In Switzerland—the best doctors in the world."

"And it doesn't worry you that...that you'll never be lovers again? I mean...physical lovers?"

"Of course it does! But all that matters now, the only thing that matters, is to get him well again, as well as can be." She fell silent for a while, and said at last with a sigh: "Yes, I'll miss the lovemaking; he was always so gentle and considerate in bed, and virile too, the most virile man in the world. It'll be hard, for both of us. But he really needs me now. And I won't desert him, ever! How could I? No. Our love is not as shallow as that, thank God!"

They were walking along under the shaded Rivoli terrace, past all the once-elegant little stores, now mostly denuded of their merchandise. Simone murmured, "Can he walk at least? Is he strong enough for a long drive to Strasbourg?"

"Oh yes. He's quite indestructible, isn't he?"

Simone nodded. "Yes, he always was; it's one of the things about him that always impressed me. I remember once..."

She was finding comfort in talk, and she went on, "A few years ago we were skiing together in St. Moritz; my husband thought I was visiting my parents in Brittany. Anyway, he took the most terrible fall, went over a cliff and fell way down to the bottom, broke both his legs and a wrist. And that very night, only a few hours after they set it all to rights for him, in his private room in the hospital, he insisted on making love to me, said he didn't see why he should have to give up all of life's little pleasures just because of a few broken bones. And in less than a week, he was walking again, he threw away his crutches because he didn't want to look like a cripple. He really is a wonderful man."

Jill nodded. "Yes, resilience is something that I've always admired too. It's one of the greatest of the virtues."

"How long have you been working for him?"

"Long enough." Jill sighed. "Long enough to...to almost fall in love with him myself, even though everything he did or said seemed deliberately designed to annoy the whole world."

They crossed over the little Place des Pyramides with its gilded equestrian statue of Joan of Arc, and into rue St. Honore, and Jill said, "If you leave within an hour or two, you'll be out of the city before the curfew begins. Where do you keep your car?"

"In the garage on St. Michel."

"I'll drive you both there."

"That's sweet of you."

"It's more of a question, I'm afraid," Jill said dryly, "of getting him off our hands."

"*Our* hands?"

"My associates. They're caring for him now."

"And you all have my undying gratitude! The love I have for that man..." She pounded her breast emotionally. "It hurts, sometimes, physically *hurts*, here."

"Oh yes," Jill said. "That's something I know a great deal about."

They came at last to *le parking B.P.*, and as they climbed the dark ramp to where Jill had parked Yvonne's car, Jill said, a little diffidently, "There's one more thing, Simone. I'm afraid you'll have to crouch down on the floor in the back of the car. I hope you don't mind."

Simone was startled. "If you say so. But why?"

"Because I can't afford to drive through the streets of Paris in the rush-hour traffic with a blindfolded passenger beside me, it would invite a lot of quite unwelcome attention."

"*Blindfold!*"

Jill sighed. "I'm taking you to a very secret place indeed, perhaps the safest safe-house in Paris. We're very strict about who knows where it is."

Simone shrugged, a very eloquent sort of gesture. "Then I have no objection whatsoever. But has it occurred to you that if I wanted to find out—which I don't—all I'd have to do is ask Miles?" She hesitated.

"Unless, of course, he was taken there blindfolded too. Yes, I suppose he must have been."

"No, as a matter of fact, he wasn't," Jill said, smiling. "But he'd never tell you."

"Oh?"

"Because he's a *professional*. It's as simple as that."

Simone fell silent, and submitted meekly when Jill tied over her eyes the napkin she had brought from Yvonne's place.

They eased their way down to the street, and Jill drove around for half an hour even though the hideout was only three short blocks away—a matter of principle. And at last the big timbered door to the restaurant delivery yard was opened by the watchman at the beep-beep of the horn, and promptly closed behind them.

Jill led Simone down the steps to the cellar, holding her arm, opened the barrel entrance, and ushered her into the hideout.

It was dark in there, only a few of the bulbs were lit, and they were all waiting—Josh Dekker and Hugh Black, Ira Watslaw, Mike Homer and Del Adam, and Yvonne Fremont too. Their guns were drawn, out of habit, at the sound of the secret door's opening, at the footsteps in the great hollow barrel.

Jill removed the blindfold and said, "Simone Delaunay, Ferret's girl, and she's a nurse, so perhaps he'll start recovering more quickly. As for what he's been up to, it's so simple we should perhaps have guessed. He was planning on absconding to Switzerland with all that money, with her too, to live happily ever after. Well, they won't have that two million francs, they'll have to start from scratch, but he's got friends there. And it will solve...solve our problems...won't it?"

Her voice was trailing away as she saw the look in Josh Dekker's eyes. She looked at Hugh, at Ira and the others, and she knew. She felt the blood leaving her face.

Josh said heavily, "He's dead, Jill. Dead."

They heard the low moan that was Simone's, and Yvonne was at her side at once as Josh went on, "An hour ago, he called out, very weakly, 'Give my love to Simone,' and when we went to him, he just reached out and groped for my hand. And then he died."

With a long, drawn-out "Aahhh..." Simone ran to the corner where the cot was, and fell to her knees beside it.

She pulled aside the white sheet that covered the body, and clutched at it, rocking back and forth and weeping her heart out. The men just stood around helplessly as Yvonne went to a cupboard and poured cognac into glasses. She took one of them to Simone, and she said gently, "Come, *ma petite*, your tears won't help him now. And his dreadful suffering is over. Take this..."

Simone looked up at the glass with red-rimmed eyes and shook her head. "No, no."

"Take it," Yvonne said firmly. "It kills all kinds of pain."

Simone climbed slowly to her feet and whispered, "He was such a good man." But she took the glass and drank it down, and Yvonne covered the body up again, reverently, and said quietly, "And what will you do now? Can you hide your tears from your husband, when he thinks you've been to the dressmaker's? It won't be easy for you."

"No, I can't, I won't, and I won't have to. I'll never see my husband again."

"And so?"

Simone bit her lip. "That money..., it was meant for the Resistance, wasn't it?"

"Yes. That's where it is now."

"And I'm glad of it."

Simone began wandering, stopping from time to time to talk directly to Jill. "Oh, I knew what we were doing was wrong, very wrong, and foolish too! But..."

She was beginning to cry again. "But the thought of Switzerland, the lakes, the mountains, the rivers, the peaceful little villages, with a man I loved so deeply. Yes, I know how wrong it was, I just didn't care."

She went to Dekker and said, very much in control of herself again, "Are you the leader here?"

"Yes, I am. The name's Josh Dekker."

"Will you tell me about the disposal of...of the body?"

"Well..." He was terribly ill at ease. He said slowly, "A graveyard's out of the question, I'm afraid, and we can't just dump him in the street—"

"I should think not!" Jill said indignantly, and Dekker went on, "We decided on the river, a weighted sack, it's the best we can do."

Simone turned away to hide her emotion, and Jill said angrily, "It is *not* the best we can do, Josh Dekker! We can bury him decently in the forest!"

Dekker threw up his arms and looked at Hugh Black, who was nodding his head. "Easy enough to do, dear boy," the ex-Major said. "And it's the *decent* thing to do."

"Okay then." He turned to Ira. "If you, Del, and Mike can borrow a German truck for us? Round about midnight, when all of Paris is asleep. Except for the enemy."

"You got it," Mike Homer said.

Jill was worried. She said quietly to Simone, a woman she was beginning to care about, "And you? What will you do now?"

"I want," Simone said clearly, "to spend the rest of my life, however short it may be, killing Germans for what they did to the man I loved."

She saw Yvonne Fremont's frown, and said, "Oh, I realize that my record is not a good one, but it's behind me now. I'm told that there are thousands of women in the Resistance, and not one of them has more cause to fight than I have."

There was a long silence, and Yvonne said at last, "It's a hard, harsh life, Simone. I don't think you'd be up to it."

"I'm a trained nurse, for God's sake! Are you telling me that the men of the Resistance are in no need of nurses?"

Yvonne Fremont turned to Dekker, "Take her with you tonight," she said, "and introduce her to Lievre."

"Okay. You don't want to come with us?"

Yvonne smiled thinly. "At midnight," she said, "I'll be very, very busy. The senior officers of the Gestapo are holding a dinner tonight, in *my* restaurant, where else? to welcome their new General."

She threw a look at Hugh Black and said, "For the officer who's replacing poor damned Hans. Every German-speaking waiter I have will be on station, and by midnight I have to be on hand to collate all the intelligence they'll be gathering, the little bits and pieces that come so easily from loose talk. If you could only see the quantity of wines and cognac they've ordered! By tomorrow, without a doubt, I'll have a great deal to tell Lievre."

"Good. I'm glad to hear it."

"Simone is right, we always need nurses. And maybe she can be taught to fight as well. Just like the rest of us. Lievre will know."

Shortly after midnight, Dekker's little party, with Simone and her dead lover aboard, left rue de la Sourdiere, the Street of the Deaf Woman, on which Yvonne's famous restaurant was situated.

As they turned the corner in their stolen Wehrmacht personnel carrier (five dead soldiers lying in Place Vendome no longer in need of it), they could hear the boisterous, drunken - singing in there, loud voices raised in the martial songs of the German Army: *Today, Germany belongs to us, Tomorrow, the whole World.*

"Over my dead body," Josh Dekker growled, as Mike Homer steered his way on the silent and almost-deserted streets of the great city, peopled now only by patrolling German soldiers, their machine pistols constantly at the ready. Some of them saw Ira Watslaw's high-ranking uniform, and snapped to a salute; most of them ignored the vehicle, one of their own.

They were on their way to the beautiful forest of Fontainebleau, more than forty thousand acres of sand and sandstone quarries, of rocks, gorges and streams, of beech trees, spruce, chestnut, hornbeam, birch, pine, and the famous oaks.

It was a forest that had once been home to kings and queens— to Philip the Fair, to Henry II, to James V of Scotland, Charles V of Germany, Christina of Sweden, Christian VII of Denmark, and Peter the Great of Russia. Pope Pius VII had consecrated the Emperor Napoleon here, and ten years later was confined here as his prisoner.

Today, it was a hideout for roving bands of the *maquis* known as *la Résistance*, and a focal point for the ruthless might of the Gestapo that relentlessly hunted them down. It was a place of blood, mayhem, and the most dreadful slaughter.

And this night, it was to become the final resting place for the tortured and desperate man named Ferret.

THE END

ABOUT THE AUTHOR

Alan Lyle-Smythe was born in Surrey, England. Prior to World War II, he served with the Palestine Police from 1936 to 1939 and learned the Arabic language. He was awarded an MBE in June 1938. He married Aliza Sverdova in 1939, then studied acting from 1939 to 1941.

In January 1940, Lyle-Smythe was commissioned in the Royal Army Service Corps. Due to his linguistic skills, he transferred to the Intelligence Corps and served in the Western Desert, in which he used the surname "Caillou" (the French word for 'pebble') as an alias.

He was captured in North Africa, imprisoned and threatened with execution in Italy, then escaped to join the British forces at Salerno. He was then posted to serve with the partisans in Yugoslavia. He wrote about his experiences in the book *The World is Six Feet Square* (1954). He was promoted to captain and awarded the Military Cross in 1944.

Following the war, he returned to the Palestine Police from 1946 to 1947, then served as a Police Commissioner in British-occupied Italian Somaliland from 1947 to 1952, where he was recommissioned a captain.

After work as a District Officer in Somalia and professional hunter, Lyle-Smythe travelled to Canada, where he worked as a hunter and then became an actor on Canadian television.

He wrote his first novel, *Rogue's Gambit*, in 1955, first using the name Caillou, one of his aliases from the war. Moving from Vancouver to Hollywood, he made an appearance as a contestant on the January 23 1958 edition of *You Bet Your Life*.

He appeared as an actor and/or worked as a screenwriter in such shows as *Daktari, The Man From U.N.C.L.E.* (including the screenwriting for *"The Bow-Wow Affair"* from 1965), *Thriller, Daniel Boone, Quark, Centennial*, and *How the West Was Won*. In 1966-67, he had a recurring role (as Jason Flood) in NBC's *"Tarzan"* TV series starring Ron Ely. Caillou appeared in such television movies as *Sole Survivor* (1970), *The Hound of the Baskervilles* (1972, as Inspector Lestrade), and *Goliath Awaits* (1981). His cinema film credits included roles in *Five Weeks in a Balloon* (1962), *Clarence, the Cross-Eyed Lion* (1965), *The Rare Breed* (1966), *The Devil's Brigade* (1968), *Hellfighters* (1968), *Everything You Always Wanted to Know About Sex* (*But Were Afraid to Ask)* (1972), *Herbie Goes to Monte Carlo* (1977), *Beyond Evil* (1980), *The Sword and the Sorcerer* (1982) and *The Ice Pirates* (1984).

Caillou wrote 52 paperback thrillers under his own name and the nom de plume of Alex Webb, with such heroes as Cabot Cain, Colonel Matthew Tobin, Mike Benasque, Ian Quayle and Josh Dekker, as well as writing many magazine stories.

Several of Caillou's novels were made into films, such as *Rampage* with Robert Mitchum in 1963, based on his big game hunting knowledge; *Assault on Agathon*, for which Caillou did the screenplay as well; and *The Cheetahs*, filmed in 1989.

He was married to Aliza Sverdova from 1939 until his death. Their daughter Nadia Caillou was the screenwriter for the film *Skeleton Coast*.

Alan Caillou died in Sedona, Arizona in 2006.

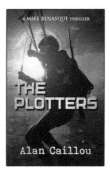

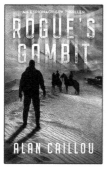

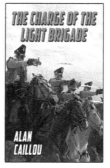

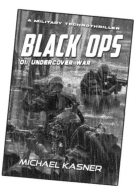

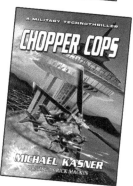

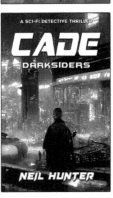

CALIBER COMICS GOES TO WAR!
HISTORICAL AND MILITARY THEMED GRAPHIC NOVELS

**WORLD WAR ONE:
MO MAN'S LAND**
ISBN: 9781635298123

*A look at World War 1 from
the French trenches as they
faced the Imperial German
Army.*

**CORTEZ AND THE FALL
OF THE AZTECS**
ISBN: 9781635299779

*Cortez battles the Aztecs
while in search of Inca
gold.*

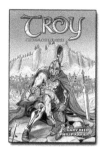

**TROY:
AN EMPIRE UNDER SIEGE**
ISBN: 9781635298635

*Homer's famous The Iliad and
the Trojan War is given a
unique human perspective
rather than from the God's.*

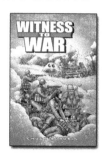

WITNESS TO WAR
ISBN: 9781635299700

*WW2's Battle of the Bulge
is seen up close by an
embedded female war
reporter.*

THE LINCOLN BRIGADE

ISBN: 9781635298222

*American volunteers head
to Spain in the 1930s to
fight in their civil war
against the fascist regime.*

**EL CID:
THE CONQUEROR**
ISBN: 9780982654996

*Europe's greatest warrior
attempts to unify Spain
against invading foreign
and domestic armies.*

WINTER WAR

ISBN: 9780985749392

*At the outbreak of WW2
Finland fights against an
invading Soviet army.*

**ZULUNATION:
END OF EMPIRE**
ISBN: 9780941613415

*The global British Empire
and far-reaching influence
is threatened by a Zulu
uprising in southern Africa.*

AIR WARRIORS: WORLD WAR ONE #V1 - V4 *Take to the skys of WW1 as various fighter aces tell their harrowing stories.*
ISBN: 9781635297973 (V1), 9781635297980 (V2), 9781635297997 (V3), 9781635298000 (V4)

ALSO AVAILABLE FROM CALIBER COMICS

QUALITY GRAPHIC NOVELS TO ENTERTAIN

THE SEARCHERS: VOLUME 1
The Shape of Things to Come

Before *League of Extraordinary Gentlemen* there was *The Searchers*. At the dawn of the 20th Century the greatest literary adventurers from the minds of Wells, Doyle, Burroughs, and Haggard were created. All thought to be the work of pure fiction. However, a century later, the real-life descendents of those famous characters are recuited by the legendary Professor Challenger in order to save mankind's future. Series collected for the first time.

"Searchers is the comic book I have on the wall with a sign reading - 'Love books? Never read a comic? Try this one! ....money back guarantee...'" - Dark Star Books.

WAR OF THE WORLDS: INFESTATION

Based on the H.G. Wells classic! The "Martian Invasion" has begun again and now mankind must fight for its very humanity. It happened slowly at first but by the third year, it seemed that the war was almost over... the war was almost lost.

"Writer Randy Zimmerman has a fine grasp of drama, and spins the various strands of the story into a coherent whole... imaginative and very gritty."
- war-of-the-worlds.co.uk

HELSING: LEGACY BORN

From writer Gary Reed (Deadworld) and artists John Lowe (Captain America), Bruce McCorkindale (Godzilla). She was born into a legacy she wanted no part of and pushed into a battle recessed deep in the shadows of the night. Samantha Helsing is torn between two worlds...two allegiances...two families. The legacy of the Van Helsing family and their crusade against the "night creatures" comes to modern day with the most unlikely of all warriors.

"Congratulations on this masterpiece..."
- Paul Dale Roberts, Compuserve Reviews

DEADWORLD

Before there was The Walking Dead there was Deadworld. Here is an introduction of the long running classic horror series, Deadworld, to a new audience! Considered by many to be the godfather of the original zombie comic with over 100 issues and graphic novels in print and over 1,000,000 copies sold, Deadworld ripped into the undead with intelligent zombies on a mission and a group of poor teens riding in a school bus desperately try to stay one step ahead of the sadistic, Harley-riding King Zombie. Death, mayhem, and a touch of supernatural evil made Deadworld a classic and now here's your chance to get into the story!

DAYS OF WRATH

Award winning comic writer & artist Wayne Vansant brings his gripping World War II saga of war in the Pacific to Guadalcanal and the Battle of Bloody Ridge. This is the powerful story of the long, vicious battle for Guadalcanal that occurred in 1942-43. When the U.S. Navy orders its ships are outnumbered and out-gunned ships to run from the Japanese fleet, they abandon American troops on a bloody, battered island in the South Pacific.

"Heavy on authenticity, compellingly written and beautifully drawn."
- Comics Buyers Guide

SHERLOCK HOLMES:
THE CASE OF THE MISSING MARTIAN

Sherlock is called out of retirement to London in 1908 to solve a most baffling mystery: The British Museum is missing a specimen of a Martian from the failed invasion of 1899. Did it walk away on its own or did someone steal it?

Holmes ponders the facts and remembers his part in the war effort alongside Professor Challenger during the War of the Worlds invasion that was chronicled in H.G. Wells' classic novel.

Meanwhile, Doctor Watson has problems of his own when his wife steals a scalpel from his surgical tool kit and returns to her old stomping grounds of Whitechapel, the London

CALIBER PRESENTS

The original Caliber Presents anthology title was one of Caliber's inaugural releases and featured predominantly new creators, many of which went onto successful careers in the comics' industry. In this new version, Caliber Presents has expanded to graphic novel size and while still featuring new creators it also includes many established professional creators with new visions. Creators featured in this first issue include nominees and winners of some of the industry's major awards including the Eisner, Harvey, Xeric, Ghastly, Shel Dorf, Comic Monsters, and more.

LEGENDLORE

From Caliber Comics now comes the entire Realm and Legendlore saga as a set of volumes that collects the long running critically acclaimed series. In the vein of The Lord of The Rings and The Hobbit with elements of Game of Thrones and Dungeon and Dragons.

Four normal modern day teenagers are plunged into a world they thought only existed in novels and film. They are whisked away to a magical land where dragons roam the skies, orcs and hobgoblins terrorize travelers, where unicorns prance through the forest, and kingdoms wage war for dominance. It is a world where man is just one race, joining other races such as elves, trolls, dwarves, changelings, and the dreaded night creatures who steal the night.

TIME GRUNTS

What if Hitler's last great Super Weapon was – Time itself! A WWII/time travel adventure that can best be described as *Band of Brothers* meets *Time Bandits*.

October, 1944. Nazi fortunes appear bleaker by the day. But in the bowels of the Wenceslas Mines, a terrible threat has emerged . . . The Nazis have discovered the ability to conquer time itself with the help of a new ominous device!

Now a rag tag group of American GIs must stop this threat to the past, present, and future . . . While dealing with their own past, prejudices, and fears in the process.

CALIBER
COMICS

www.calibercomics.com

Milton Keynes UK
Ingram Content Group UK Ltd.
UKHW020914220424
441551UK00017B/1145